Cougar II Triangle of Lust

Alejandro Morales

Published by Alejandro Morales, 2014.

Neil,

Enjoy!

Alejandro Morales

COUGAR II TRIANGLE OF LUST

First edition. November 10, 2014.

Copyright © 2014 Alejandro Morales.

Written by Alejandro Morales.

I'd like to dedicate this book to all of the readers that believe in me and have supported me. Without you, my voice, my vision could not be expressed. A special thank you to Anne Rice, thank you for your support and my father, Benito Morales for providing the artwork for the cover.

I The Contender

"Rodriguez is taking a beating in there! Die-hard fight fans knew that Rodriguez wasn't ready for this level of competition!" the announcer says. Nick is standing against the fence of the octagon as his opponent is trying to strike him. "Samuel has Rodriguez against the cage and is hitting him with knees and elbows to the head! If Rodriguez doesn't defend himself or get off of the cage, the referee will have to stop the fight" the announcer says. Luis looks at Nick's attempts to block Samuel's blows and shouts, "Dammit Nick! Get off of the fucking cage! Block his knees, grab him and try to spin him around!"

Luis looks back at the corner men and shouts, "Fuck! It's like he forgot everything we did during training camp! What the fuck is going on?" The corner men shrug their shoulders and don't answer Luis' question. Luis returns his focus on to the octagon and winces as Nick is hit. Samuel continues to throw elbows at Nick's head as the referee says to Nick, "Defend yourself or I'm stopping the fight!"

Anna stands up from her couch and yells at her television. "Nick, fight back! You're going to lose! Please baby, fight back!" Anna begins to cry s she witnesses the one-sided assault that Nick is involved in. "I wish I could be there in person, but Nick insisted that I don't go. Ever since the day of Sam's funeral, we had to keep our relationship a secret. We don't go out in public together, we have to sneak around to see each other. God forbid Luis ever found out about us. Who knows how he would react. Even my girlfriends don't know about Nick" Anna thought.

Anna turns her attention back to the television and sees the referee getting ready to step between Nick and Samuel to stop the fight. The bell mercifully rings and the referee separates the fighters since the round has ended. Anna looks at the television and says, "Nick baby, please do something! I don't want you to lose! You worked so hard for this fight! You can't afford to lose this fight! Please baby do something!"

Nick slowly goes into his corner and sees the look on Luis' face that he has seen before. Luis is angered by Nick's lack of offense and wants this changed immediately. Nick sits on the stool in his corner of the octagon and the cut man treats Nick's wounds. The cut man focuses on the cut Nick has under his left eye from one of elbows that Samuel hit him with.

Blood flows from the gash under Nick's eye as the cut man treats the wound. A cameraman sees Nick's wound and focuses his camera on to Nick's face for the audience to see. Anna sees the gash under Nick's eye and starts to cry. The crowd attending the fight gasp at the sight of the gash under Nick's eye. Luis motions for the cameraman to leave and focuses his attention on to Nick.

Luis gets on one knee in front of Nick and says, "Nick, what the fuck is going on? You're not doing anything we prepared for in camp! You have to stick to the plan! This guy is ahead of you on points and you have to knock him out or make him tap out to win! You worked too hard for this shot to give up now! Whatever is going on in your head needs to go away! Nick, protect your eye, take Samuel down and ground and pound him or go for the choke if you see an opening. I know you can do this! Focus!"

The cut man finishes treating the gash under Nick's eye and gives Luis a thumbs up. He leaves the octagon and Nick leans his head back so one of the corner men can give him some water. An image of Anna enters his mind as he drinks the water. Anna is standing in front of him completely nude. She walks up to Nick and says, "I only fuck winners. Sam was a winner. Do this for me. If you want me, win!" Nick quickly returns his attention back to Luis and says, "Yes coach!" and gets up from the stool.

Luis and the corner men leave the octagon as the third and final round of the fight is going to begin. "Ladies and Gentlemen, I'm Joe Gordon here with my colleague Mark Smith and we are going into round three of this Heavyweight fight. I don't know what Luis said to Rodriguez, but he looks fired up! Rodriguez is a 150 to 1 underdog in this fight, ranked number ten in the Heavyweight division. Samuel is currently ranked number two in the World. Samuel has dominated this fight since the first round. I've never seen Rodriguez fight this badly. It's as if he's not here and his mind is elsewhere" Joe says.

Mark chimes in and says, "We all know that he can take a beating and dish it out, but this fight has become a one-sided beating. Rodriguez is facing a guy that I personally feel that he's not ready for. He needs some more fights under his belt before trying to get into the top 5 rankings, especially against the number two contender. The murder of Sam Gonzalez rocked the sports world and left us without a champion for a while. The belt was awarded to the number one contender, John 'Stone Hands' Walden. Walden was supposed to face Sam Gonzalez for the title, but that obviously never happened. I honestly believe that Rodriguez got this fight because of the emotions surrounding Gonzalez' murder and his desire to win the title in honor of his teammate and friend. I think that Rodriguez let his emotions get the better of him and it may cost him tonight."

Joe looks at Mark and says, "Mark, I agree with most of what you're saying, but don't count Rodriguez out yet. Emotion has shown to be a strength, not a weakness for him. Rodriguez has a lot of heart and add the fact that Luis is in his corner, who we all know is the master motivator, I think that Rodriguez could pull this off. If Rodriguez loses, trust me, Luis will make sure that he learns from this, regroups and comes back." "Let's all hope so for Rodriguez' sake. OK Ladies and Gentlemen, round three is about to begin" Mark says.

Nick walks over to the middle of the octagon to begin the third and final round of the fight. The referee stands between the fighters and says, "Fighters, this is the final round. Touch gloves and come out fighting." Nick and Samuel touch gloves and Samuel says, "You're going down! That belt will be mine!" Nick looks at Samuel and says, "I don't think so" and goes back to his corner. The referee signals the beginning of the round and Samuel runs towards Nick to strike him with a flying knee.

Nick avoids Samuel's attack and quickly grabs Samuel by the waist. Samuel tries to throw an elbow at Nick's head and Nick avoids it. He punches Nick several times in the head and Nick thought, "I have him now!" Nick lifts Samuel's body over his head and slams it into the canvas of the octagon. The crowd erupts with cheers at the sight of a perfectly executed suplex that makes Samuel's head bounce off of the octagon canvas.

"Oh my God! Did you see that? Samuel's head crashed into the canvas off of Rodriguez' perfectly executed suplex! This is something we've never seen him do before! You would have to go back to the days of Dan "The Beast" Severn to see a suplex like that! Samuel is in major trouble!" Joe says. Samuel struggles to get up from the canvas as Nick looks at him. Nick gets up from the canvas and immediately wraps his arms around Samuel's exposed neck to apply a choke hold.

Samuel tries to separate Nick's arms to break to hold, but Nick leans back, tightening the hold. Samuel punches Nick in the head and stomach to no avail. Luis shouts, "You got him kid! Tighten up!" Nick tightens his grip and Samuel struggles to breathe. He becomes light-headed and is forced to tap Nick's forearm to signal that he submits to Nick's choke hold.

The crowd erupts as the referee steps in between Nick and Samuel to break up the choke hold. Nick slowly stands up and raises his arms up in victory as blood flows from the cut beneath his left eye. Anna jumps up from her couch in excitement. "Yes!

You did it baby! You did it! Thank God! I hope Nick's OK" she shouts.

Tears of joy roll down from Anna's eyes and she smiles. "I knew he could do it. Even Luis had his doubts, but I knew my man can win! God did he look so good tonight! Nick had to train so hard for this fight, he looks like he was carved out of stone. His arms, his legs, his abs, yes I can finally say abs, he lost that gut he had, umm...I can't wait for him to get back here. I'm going to give him a special treat" she thought with a smile.

Luis enters the octagon along with the cut man so they can attend to Nick. "Nick, can you see out of that eye?" the cut man asks. "It's a little blurry" Nick says. Luis takes a hold of Nick and helps him walk towards the center of the octagon. "I'm proud of you kid! You stood in there, took everything Samuel had and beat him! You're the next champ!" Luis says. Nick smiles and says, "Thanks coach" and goes to the referee.

The referee raises Nick's hand as the announcer addresses the crowd. "Ladies and Gentlemen. The winner by tap out via rear-naked choke and NEW number one contender for the Heavyweight Championship of the World, Nick "Hard Head" Rodriguez!" The referee lowers Nick's arm and Luis hugs Nick. Luis whispers, "You're the next Champ kid" and Nick smiles. The crowd cheers and Joe enters the octagon to interview Nick.

Ana returns to her couch and listens intently to Nick's interview. "That was amazing. I thought Nick was going to lose this fight, but he won. I hope he's OK. I wonder what he's going to say," she thought. Nick has some difficulty standing upright and leans on Luis for support. "Nick! Once again you show us that you should not be underestimated and score this huge upset over Samuel. How were you able to take all of that punishment and come back to hit a beautiful suplex on Samuel then choke him out?" Joe asks.

Nick stands upright and Luis moves back so Nick can answer Joe's question. Nick smiles and says, "Joe, that's the problem.

When everyone thinks that I can't do something, I prove them wrong. I'm not called 'Hard Head' for nothing. Samuel hits like a fucking mule! Whoops...sorry about that" Nick says. Joe and the crowd chuckle and Nick says, "Samuel hits really hard and I thought that I was going to lose, but thinking about a very special lady in my life made me come back and win."

Luis looks at Nick with a look of concern after he answers Joe's questions. He thought, "Oh shit, not this again! I had to deal with this shit with Sam and now Nick! I bet he was thinking about this girl instead of the fight. I can't have my fighters being distracted like this! Nick almost lost tonight and got hurt! I'll talk to him later about this." Nick smiles and says, "She's not here tonight, but I know she's watching at home. Baby, I'm coming home and I love you!" Anna smiles at the television and says, "I love you too."

Nick, Luis and the corner men leave the octagon and go back to the locker room. Nick is trying to walk in a straight line as he holds his head in pain and his vision is blurred. He has difficulty concentrating and staggers as he walks. One of the corner men tap Luis on the shoulder and point to Nick so Luis can observe how Nick is walking. Luis looks at Nick and is very concerned.

Luis turns to Nick and Nick stops walking. Luis says, "As soon as we get to the locker room, I want the doctor to check you out." Nick says, "OK" and slowly walks with Luis. They walk into the locker room and Nick hears his phone ringing from his locker. "That's probably Anna. She's probably calling me to see how I'm doing or congratulate me. I can't answer her call with Luis here. Only a few close friends know about my relationship with Anna and that would kill Luis. I'll let it go to voicemail and call her later" he thought.

Luis hears Nick's phone ringing and asks, "Are you going to get that? The doctor won't be here for a few minutes so you might as well answer it now." Nick sheepishly reaches for his phone and tries to hide the image of Anna on his phone's screen from Luis. He presses the Answer button on his phone and says, "Hi hon! No, I'm OK, just a little dizzy, but I'll be OK. The doctor is going to take a look at me, so I'll call you when he's done. OK honey, love you too."

Nick quickly puts his phone away as Luis looks at Nick with a puzzled look. "The girl on Nick's phone looked a little familiar. I saw a little bit of her face, but it's as if Nick didn't want anyone to see his phone. That's not like him. Ever since Sam's funeral, he hasn't been the same. I've been meaning to have a talk with him, but he's been avoiding any one-on-one talks with me. It's been all business" Luis thought. At the conclusion of Luis' thought, the doctor enters the locker room and examines Nick.

Nick sits upright so the doctor can examine him. The doctor looks at Nick's left eye and notices the broken blood vessels in his eye. "Nick, I want you to close your right eye and tell me how clearly you can see" he says. Nick closes his right eye and the entire room becomes a blur. He can't tell where the doctor is seated as there are three images of the doctor in front of him.

Nick is paralyzed in fear and grabs the doctor's arm. "Oh shit doc! My eye is fucked up! I see three of you!" Nick shouts. Nick is frozen in fear as Luis rushes over to him and says, "Everything will be OK. Doc has dealt with this before and will make you better." Luis' words make Nick feel at ease and he lets go of the doctor's arm. The doctor says, "Thank you" to Luis and he says, "No problem."

Nick looks at the doctor in fear, almost on the verge of crying. The doctor says, "I want you in my office tomorrow so we can do some thorough testing. Based on what I'm seeing now, I don't want you driving and no strenuous activity." Nick frowns, turns to Luis and asks, "Luis, can I talk to the doc in private for a moment?" Luis nods his head and walks away.

Nick waits for Luis to walk away and asks, "Doc, is it really bad? Is my eye going to get better? I can't have my career end like this! I've never been hurt like this before. To be honest, I've never been this scared for a long time. Doc, please tell me that this will heal and I can continue to fight. When you say 'strenuous activity' does that include sex?"

The doctor looks at Nick and laughs. He says, "You young guys! You have a legitimate issue with your eye and you're concerned about sex! I know that you want to celebrate your win tonight, but that's not going to happen. No sex, no exercise of any kind, don't even submerge your head in water, so no swimming or relaxing in the tub." Nick frowns at says, "Yes doc."

The doctor continues to examine Nick. He says, "You need rest. See me tomorrow at 9am at my office and prepare to be there for a few hours. I want to take no chances with your eye. Frankly, you're lucky you don't have a concussion." Nick frowns and says, "Yes doc, I'll see you tomorrow. First thing in the morning. Thanks." The doctor leaves and Nick struggles to stand.

Nick leans on the locker in front of him and begins to cry. The tears from his eyes trickle down into the gash under his left eye and he winces from the stinging sensation he feels. "Fuck that stings!" he shouts.

Nick punches the locker, leaving a large dent in it. He shouts, "Fuck!" and struggles to stand as he begins to feel dizzy and light-headed. Nick wipes away his tears and places his back against the locker, looking up at the ceiling. The glare from the ceiling lights temporarily blind Nick and he turns his head around to avoid looking at the lights.

Nick sighs as he tries to stand. The room begins to spin and Nick closes his eyes so he can regain his equilibrium. He opens his eyes and thought, "If I wasn't thinking about the argument I had with Anna last week before I left for Vegas, I wouldn't be here now! She's so fucking demanding at times! I told her that I'm not ready to tell everyone about us and she doesn't care."

Nick struggles to lean against a locker. The room continues to spin and he thought, "It's like she doesn't give a fuck that people still mourn Sam's death and if I went out in public with her that could lead to more problems. Sometimes I wish that I didn't see Anna in the shower that day."

Nick sits on a bench next to the locker. As he tries to regain his equilibrium, he whispers, "I betrayed my friend by fucking his woman. It wasn't supposed to happen, but it did. I let my dick do my thinking for me and fucked Anna on the day of Sam's funeral! I hate feeling this way! I love Anna! She makes me feel special and does things that no other woman has ever done to me before. Eventually we'll tell everyone that we're together, but not now..." Nick's body collapses to the floor and all Nick sees is Luis' concerned face as he yells for help.

II In Memorium

"Here we lay the body of Samuel Gonzalez into the ground. Samuel was a passionate young man who lived his life to the fullest and leaves behind a world that will miss him dearly. Samuel was taken from us too early in his life, but has left his mark on all of us. Do not mourn Samuel's passing, but celebrate his life, what he has done, how he has touched as all as a person, as a fighter, as a champion" the priest says.

Sam's relatives, Luis, Nick, Anna, Susan, Miriam and Jane all weep as the priest performs his sermon. The mourners' cries can be heard from the far side of the cemetery as the priest speaks. Anna leans against Nick's chest as she sobs. He holds Anna close to his body as he tries to console her. Tears stream from Nick's eyes as he looks at the casket that Sam will soon be buried in.

The priest closes his bible and looks at the mourners. He says, "If anyone would like to say some final words for Samuel, please came forward." The mourners look at each other to see who will speak. After a brief moment of silence, Luis slowly walks over to the large portrait of Sam that is displayed by the casket.

Luis tries to compose himself and wipes away his tears. "Sam is, was the son I never had. I knew him since he was a kid, getting into trouble and fights. He came into my gym one day and ever since that day, we were friends. Sam...Sam...he...I can't believe he's gone..." Luis sobbingly says and begins to cry uncontrollably. Luis' cries resonate throughout the cemetery. The other mourners begin to sob loudly, bringing the priest and cemetery employees to tears.

Nick composes himself and goes over to Luis to console him. He and leads Luis away from the casket so other mourners can speak. Anna turns her head to see where Nick is taking Luis. Luis leans on Nick, crying and bawling uncontrollably. A wave of guilt and sadness takes over Anna's emotions and she cries uncontrollably. Anna cries for several minutes as she watches Luis and regains her composure.

Anna wipes her tears and looks at Sam's casket. "It's not fair! Why did Paul kill Sam! Sam was so young and full of life! He had it all and Paul just came and ended it! He kills Sam and almost killed me! Oh my God! I betrayed Sam again! I slept with his friend! I fucked Nick! Jesus Christ, what the fuck is wrong with me? Why did I do that? Is it because Nick reminds me of Sam? I don't know what I'm thinking. I just don't want to be alone, especially now. Nick is so kind and caring. If he didn't help me that day, I'd be dead. This is so confusing" Anna thought.

Nick walks back over to Anna and says, "I just got Luis to calm down. He's really upset about Sam. Luis really loved Sam and he can't bear the pain of Sam's death." Luis walks over to his car and stops to look back at the crowd of mourners. He tearfully says, "I love you Sam" and the driver opens the door for him. Luis enters the car and quickly closes the door so no one can hear his cries.

Anna leans on Nick's chest and says, "I know how he feels" and cries. Nick tearfully says, "Me too" and holds Anna close to his body. The priest concludes his sermon and says, "Let's say our final farewell to Samuel and let us go in peace and love from our Lord and Savior, Jesus Christ." The crowd says "Amen" and line up to toss a rose on to Sam's casket before it is lowered into the ground.

As the mourners line up, Anna and Nick embrace to console each other. Tears flow from their eyes and Anna's tears stain Nick's white shirt. Nick loosens his embrace and he leads Anna towards the casket to get a rose. Anna wipes away her tears and tries to compose herself. She reaches for a rose and pricks her finger from one of the thorns from the rose. A trickle of blood rolls down Anna's finger and the sight of blood brings a flood of images into her mind. Anna is reminded of several violent events that she witnessed while Sam was alive. An image of blood flying from Thompson's mouth after Sam punches him and an image of Brad lying in a pool of his own blood after Sam beat him enters her mind. More images enter Anna's mind as she tries to block them out.

Anna begins to tremble from these images and exhales to calm herself. As she tries to block them out, another image of blood dripping from Sam's hands enters her mind. An image of Sam lying in a pool of his own blood after Paul shot him also enters Anna's mind. She finally blocks the images and stops trembling. Anna looks at Sam's casket and pauses. She takes the rose and tosses it on to Sam's casket whispering, "I'm sorry. I will always love you" and walks away to the side.

Nick reaches for a rose and pauses in front of Sam's casket. He remembers the day that Sam was shot. Sam and Luis are training in the dojo and reporters are asking them questions. Anna watches Sam as he trains and she smiles as he hits the bag and poses for pictures. A loud firecracker sound is heard from the entrance of the dojo and Sam's head is knocked back.

A stream of blood shoots out of Sam's head and another shot is fired. Anna collapses to the ground and everyone runs away. A pool of blood surrounds Sam's and Anna's bodies as Paul fires a third time, killing himself. The image of Sam lying in a pool of his own blood lingers in Nick's mind for a moment then fades away. Nick looks at Sam's casket and feels guilty about what took place before the funeral.

Nick walks out from the bathroom in Anna's house and heads towards the stairs. "I really needed to go! This diet is killing me! All of this water that I've been drinking has made me piss like a race horse! The sound of water from Anna's bathroom didn't help either. Speaking of shower, I think I just heard her stop. I'll go back downstairs and wait for her to get dressed" he thought.

As Nick walks towards the stairs, he pauses by Anna's bedroom and can see Anna stepping out of the shower. "Holy shit! This is the last thing I wanted to see today! Anna's getting out of the shower and I'm standing here like a horny pervert staring at her! Damn she looks good! Her legs, her ass, flat stomach, her breasts...wow! Sam was a lucky mother fucker being with her. Then again, he wasn't so lucky..." When Nick finishes his thought, he sees Anna looking at him.

Nick is embarrassed that Anna caught him staring at her. "Fuck! Dammit Nick! What the fuck is wrong with you? You're staring at Sam's girl! I don't think she'll ever forgive me for this" Nick thought. Anna looks at Nick and thought, "Has Nick been standing there staring at me all this time or walked by as I was getting out of the shower? I did kiss him earlier, but I didn't think that he'd try to do something. I'm embarrassed and turned on at the same time."

Nick steps back from the doorway, holding his hand in front of his face to block his view. "Anna I'm so sorry. I didn't mean to stare at you. I came up here to use the bathroom and you stepped out of the shower as I was heading towards the stairs. When I saw you there I couldn't resist looking at you. Anna, I know you hear this a lot, but it's true. You are very beautiful and any man that can say he's your man is a lucky man. You're what's known as a timeless beauty" Nick says. Anna walks over to Nick completely nude and says, "I owe you so much. Please hold me."

Holding Anna close to his body arouses Nick and he can't resist the urge to kiss Anna. They kiss passionately and when Anna smiles and says, "We have plenty of time" Nick smiles and kisses Anna, fondling her buttocks and breasts. Anna slowly moves her hand towards Nick's penis and massages his penis as it becomes erect.

Nick steps away from Anna and takes off his blazer and his shoes. As Nick starts to take off his tie, Anna steps toward him and kisses Nick on the lips. She grabs his tie and leads Nick towards the bed, pushing him so he falls on to the mattress. Nick's body tenses as Anna lies on top of him. He looks up at the ceiling as he removes his tie and unbuttons his shirt. "This is so fucking wrong! It's not too late to stop this. I can't betray Sam like this!" he thought.

Anna removes Nick's pants and boxer shorts, exposing his erect penis. She looks at his penis and thought, "Nick needs to do a little manscaping. There's too much hair down there. If he didn't have a big dick, I wouldn't find it in all of that hair" she thought. Anna caresses Nick's penis and begins to lick the top of it. Nick says, "Anna we should..." and stops speaking when Anna inserts Nick's penis into her mouth.

A single tear comes from Nick's eye as Anna moves her head up and down his penis. Nick whispers, "Sam, I'm sorry" and leans his head back on the mattress, arching his back to adjust his body. Anna moves her hand towards Nick's testicles and fondles them while she licks the top of Nick's penis, slowly moving her tongue across it while Nick moans. Nick turns his head and looks at the clock next to the bed. He says, "Anna...Anna...we have to stop. Anna...please stop."

Anna removes Nick's penis from her mouth. She looks at him and asks, "What's wrong? Why do you want me to stop? I thought you liked me." Nick says, "Anna, we're going to be late for the funeral. We have to get going." Anna says, "OK. You're right. Let me get dressed and we'll go." Anna gets up from the bed and goes into the bathroom. Nick looks at Anna as she walks towards the bathroom. "My God she's hot!" he thought.

Nick sits up on the bed and starts to button up his shirt. "I don't believe this! I'm going to fuck my best friend's girlfriend on the day of his funeral. I'm a fucking scumbag! OK...I didn't fuck her, all I got was a blowjob. Even then, that's wrong! I'll tell

Anna that this is wrong and I can't do this. But...Anna is so fucking hot! My God, she could have been a model! Her body is so perfect and feels so good when I hold her next to me. She also gives great head. I almost came when her tongue hit the middle of the tip of my dick. I never had a woman suck my dick like that! Damn this sucks!" he thought.

Anna enters the bathroom and turns on the water from the faucet. She splashes cold water on to her face, cupping her hands under the water so she can put some water into her mouth. Anna gargles the water in her mouth, spits it out and when she stands up, sees Sam standing behind her. Anna is paralyzed in fear and looks at Sam in the mirror. "You fucking slut! You can't keep your mouth off of a dick for one day? You give my friend, my brother a blowjob on my funeral day? You disgust me!" Sam says.

Anna is frozen in fear as Sam speaks. She whispers, "He's not here. He's not here." When Anna turns around to speak, Sam is gone. "Anna we have to leave!" Nick shouts from the bedroom and Anna realizes she's still standing in front of the sink with the water running. "I feel so bad! I betrayed Sam again! I don't know what I'm doing! Sam, please forgive me" Anna thought. She turns of the water, goes into the bedroom and sees Nick standing there, fully clothed.

Anna looks at Nick as he stands in front of her with his head looking down in shame. Anna says, "Nick, I..." and Nick interrupts her. "Anna, what we did is wrong. We can't do this, not to Sam. As much as I want you, I can't betray Sam any more. I'll call the driver and ask him to wait for us so you can get dressed. We'll go to the funeral and let's leave it like that." Anna nods her head and Nick goes downstairs. Anna quickly puts on her clothes and runs downstairs. She puts on her shoes, leaning on Nick to keep her balance. Anna can feel Nick's chest as she leans on him and is impressed by how muscular it is. She looks at Nick and he avoids looking at her, staring at the floor.

Nick opens the door for Anna and they leave the house. The driver is standing outside of the car holding open the passenger door for Nick and Anna. They enter the car and Anna looks at Nick. She sees that he is crying and she wipes away a tear from his face. Nick says, "Thank you" and smiles. Anna holds Nick's hand and says, "Nick, I completely understand what you said earlier and I agree."

Nick avoids looking at Anna as she continues to speak. "I guess all of the emotions that we've got going on in our heads got the best of us. It's just so hard dealing with all of this at the same time. Sam's murder, Paul's suicide, I almost died, it's too much!" she says. Nick looks at Anna and sees that her eyes are watering. Anna cries uncontrollably and Nick holds her to console her.

The memories of what happened earlier fade away as Nick looks at Sam's casket and weeps. He takes the rose and tosses it on to the casket whispering, "I'm sorry Sam. Please forgive me. I love you bro." Nick stands by Sam's casket and stares at it. "This is so surreal. I can't believe that Sam is dead!" he thought. Nick looks at the casket as it is lowered into the ground and sobs. "He's really gone... he's really gone" Nick whispers.

Nick turns away as dirt is being thrown on to the casket. He wipes away his tears and walks over to Anna. Anna stands in front of Sam's portrait and stares at it. She whispers, "I'm sorry" and is interrupted when Nick asks, "Are you ready to go?" Anna tearfully looks at Sam's portrait and the pile of dirt where Sam is buried. She says, "Goodbye Sam, I love you." Anna turns to Nick and says, "Let's go."

Nick escorts Anna to the car and they slowly enter it. Nick sits next to Anna and she leans on his shoulder. "Thank you for everything. You've been so supportive and helpful during this whole ordeal. I'm sorry about earlier..." Anna says as Nick interrupts her. "Anna, I'm just as guilty as you are. I should have never stared at you. I should have resisted touching you, kissing you and feeling the way I feel about you."

Anna holds Nick's hand and he holds her close to his body. The warmth from Nick's body puts Anna at ease. She leans over some more, moving her head on top of Nick's chest. Nick resists the urge to make Anna sit upright and allows her to lean on his chest. "I can't continue doing this. I know she's in pain, so I have to be delicate how I treat her. No matter what, I can't be with her" Nick thought.

The car pulls up to Anna's house and the driver parks the car. Nick turns to Anna and asks, "Will you be OK?" Anna pauses as she's going to open the door and says, "I don't know. All I know is that I don't want to be alone now." Nick looks at Anna and says, "I can stick around for a little while if you want...to keep you company, of course." Anna smiles and says, "OK" and opens the door.

Nick leaves the car with Anna and closes the door. Nick gives the driver a tip and says, "I'll get a cab home or something, thanks." The driver says, "No problem sir you take care" and leaves the driveway. Nick looks at Anna as she stands in front of her house and can't stop looking at her. "My God, she's so beautiful. Stop it Nick! You never should have said 'OK' to her. Now what do I do?" he thought.

Anna opens the front door to the house and they enter. Nick immediately goes over to the couch and sits. Anna closes the door behind her and sees Nick sitting on the couch. Anna sits next to Nick and nervously smiles at him. There was an uncomfortable silence between them as Nick tries to avoid any eye contact with Anna. Anna breaks the silence by asking, "Do you want a drink? I could use one." Nick says, "Yes, what do you have?" Anna walks over to the refrigerator and sees a couple of beers that Paul bought the night of Sam's last fight.

Anna stares at the cans of beer and remembers what occurred that night. "Sam came here after he won his fight and beat the shit out of Paul. He beat Paul worse than Brad. Sam let Paul punch him and he laughed! Sam knocked Paul out and brought me upstairs, having his way with me. At first, I resisted, but then I couldn't stop enjoying myself. Sam's muscular body, his passion, his intensity, his big dick just turned me on. I was so turned on, I came several times when we fucked. Then that fucking pyscho Paul comes and shoots us. I wish Sam was still here. I miss him so much!" Anna thought.

Anna grabs the cans of beer and brings them into the living room. She notices that Nick took off his blazer, revealing his muscular upper body. Anna stares at Nick for a moment and thought, "Damn, Nick is really in shape. I already know that he has a big dick, not as big as Paul's or Sam's, but I'd love to know how he uses it. Holy shit! What are you thinking Anna? You and Nick talked about this! I just...ugh! I don't want to be alone! I don't want to be in this house by myself! I can't bear to be alone!"

Anna walks over to Nick and hands him a beer. Nick takes the beer and says, "Thanks." He takes a sip from the beer and leans forward to place the can on the table. As Nick leans forward, Anna leans over and kisses him on the lips. Nick places the can of beer on the coffee table and says, "Anna, I can't do this" and Anna kisses Nick on the lips again. She whispers, "Please, I don't want to be alone. Just kiss me" and kisses Nick again. Nick moves away from Anna and thought, "Oh what the fuck! I can only resist so much!" He leans towards Anna and kisses her.

Nick and Anna kiss passionately for several minutes. Anna slowly caresses Nick's face and body as she slides her body on top of his. Nick moves his hands up and down Anna's body as they kiss. Anna begins to take off her dress as Nick starts to take off his shoes, then his pants. Anna removes her dress, revealing a black bra with matching thong, instantly arousing Nick.

Anna begins to move her hand towards Nick's penis. She puts her hand inside of his boxer shorts, much to Nick's delight. Anna fondles Nick's penis until it is completely erect and it sticks out of his boxer shorts. Anna moves her body towards Nick's penis and places it into her mouth. Anna begins to move her head up and down Nick's penis while Nick takes off his shirt and tries to remove Anna's bra as she sucks on his penis.

Nick looks at Anna and smiles. "This is so wrong!" he thought as he fumbles with the snap on the back of Anna's bra. After a couple of failed attempts to remove Anna's bra, he finally removes it. Nick stares at Anna's breasts, looking at them as they bounce up and down. "Holy shit! Anna's tits look so good! I'm sorry Sam, but I can't resist" Nick thought. Anna stops sucking on Nick's penis and removes his boxer shorts so he's completely naked. Nick adjusts his body so he's sitting upright on the couch and Anna gets on her knees in front of Nick.

Anna places Nick's penis back into her mouth. Nick moans in ecstasy as he feels Anna's tongue and lips move up and down his penis. "Don't cum yet, don't cum yet" Nick thought as he squeezes the armrest on the couch. Nick's penis is completely inside of Anna's mouth as he ejaculates. Anna can taste Nick's thick, salty semen in her mouth and almost gags from the taste.

Anna slowly lifts her head from Nick's penis. Nick stares at Anna as she swallows the semen that is in her mouth. She looks at Nick and he says in embarrassment, "I'm sorry I came in your mouth. I don't normally cum that fast." Anna chuckles and says, "That's OK. As long as you have some left for later" and winks at him. Nick smiles and leans his head back as Anna puts his penis back into her mouth. As Nick leans his head back, he sees Sam standing behind him. Before Nick can speak, Sam says, "You fucking piece of shit!" and punches Nick, making the room go dark.

III Trouble in Paradise

"Get the doctor! Where's the doctor?" Luis shouts as he holds Nick's body. The doctor runs over to Luis and asks, "What happened? I just examined him and Nick was cleared to go home!" Luis tearfully says, "I don't know doc! He was standing one minute, the next minute he's on the floor." The doctor checks Nick's pulse and makes sure that he's breathing.

Nick starts to move and whispers, "Sam, I'm sorry. I'm so sorry. If I could go back and stop what happened, I would. I didn't mean for this to happen." Luis looks at Nick and the doctor in confusion. Luis asks, "What is he talking about" and the doctor says, "He must be delirious. The stretcher is on the way. We'll take him to the hospital and run some tests on him immediately."

Luis is confused and relieved at the same time. "Thank God Nick is alive! I honestly thought he was dead. What's this shit about Sam? 'I didn't mean for this to happen.' What is he talking about? I'll find out later" he thought. Nick is placed on to a stretcher and very weakly motions for Luis to come towards him. Luis jogs over to Nick as he's lying on the stretcher and leans in closely to hear him.

Nick struggles to speak as Luis leans towards him. Nick says, "Luis, I need you to call Anna and let her know where I am. She'll be worried." Luis is confused and asks, "Nick, are you sure you mean Anna? Don't you mean someone else?" Nick grabs Luis' hand and says, "No, I meant Anna! Take my phone, call her and let her know where I am! I'll explain everything later." Luis is speechless as the EMTs place on oxygen mask over Nick's face and lift the stretcher into an ambulance.

The doctor gets into the ambulance with Nick and Luis starts to cry. Luis looks at the doctor and says, "Go ahead, I'll meet you at the hospital." The doctor nods his head, closes the door and the ambulance speeds off to the hospital. Luis slowly walks over to Nick's locker and can't believe what he just heard. "What does that mean? 'I meant Anna! I'll explain later!' What the fuck is going on here? Is Nick seeing Anna? No, he couldn't."

Luis opens Nick's locker and collects Nick's belongings. Luis pauses when he sees Nick's phone. He says, "He couldn't betray Sam like that! He wouldn't do that to Sam! They were brothers! They knew each other since they were kids! Sam brought Nick into the gym after I took him in and they've been with me since. Is this why Nick's been so distracted? Is he hiding a relationship with Anna from me? This is too much!"

Luis continues to stare at Nick's gym bag. He stares at the bag for a moment and takes out Nick's cell phone. Luis sees "10 missed calls" displayed on the screen, all of them from Anna. "Jesus Christ, please tell me that they are just friends, nothing more. I can't deal with this shit!" he says. Luis looks at Nick's phone and presses the Call button on the screen from one of Anna's missed calls. "Please tell me this isn't happening. Not this!" Luis thought.

Anna is sitting at the edge of her bed, eagerly waiting for Nick's call. "I hope he's OK. Nick took a real beating tonight and he didn't look too good when he left the octagon. He had to lean on Luis to walk over to the referee. Why hasn't he returned any of my calls? Please God, let Nick be OK. Please..." she thought as her phone rings.

Anna jumps with excitement off of her bed and reaches for her phone, almost dropping it. She sees Nick's picture displayed on the screen and smiles. "Oh thank God, he's OK!" she thought. Anna presses the Answer button on the screen and quickly places the phone to her ear. She says, "Nick, Nick honey! Are you OK? Oh my God, I was so worried! I thought that something happened to you after the fight."

Luis is in shock as he listens to Anna speak. The tone of her voice worries him. "I can't believe this! Nick is seeing Anna! That's the voice of a concerned girlfriend, not someone who's just a friend. Jesus Christ! What do I do here?" Luis thought. Anna eagerly waits for a reply and asks, "Nick? Nick? Are you still there? Can you hear me baby? I love you." Hearing Anna say 'I love you' on the phone confirms his fears.

Luis looks at Nick's phone in disgust and has to pause for a moment to calm himself. His right hand turns into a fist and he punches a locker, leaving a large dent in the door. Luis exhales and breathes deeply, attempting to calm himself. After several deep breaths, Luis' heart rate returns to normal. He looks at Nick's phone and whispers, "Fucking bitch!" Luis places the phone next to his ear and exhales.

Anna eagerly waits for an answer as Luis calms himself. Luis exhales again and says, "Anna, its Luis. Nick asked me to call you. I don't know what is going on between the two of you, but he wanted me to call you. Nick is on his way to the hospital. We don't know what is wrong with him. The doctor is going to run some tests on him." Anna is in a state of shock. She stops breathing for a moment and has to clear her throat before speaking. "Luis, how is Nick? What hospital is he going to? Do you think he'll be OK?" she asks.

Luis punches the locker again, leaving a larger dent in the door and exhales. "This fucking bitch! It's bad enough that she got involved with Sam and because of her he's dead, now she's fucking his friend! His brother! This fucking cunt!" Luis thought. Luis places the phone back to his ear and says, "I think Nick will be OK. He's going to Saint Mary's Hospital which is close to the arena. I have to go now." Luis ends the call and walks away.

Anna starts to speak as Luis abruptly ends the call. Anna looks at her phone in disbelief and shouts, "You mother fucker!" She puts her phone down and starts to cry. Anna sobs and shouts, "Nick! My poor Nick! Please God, let him be OK! I can't lose another man I love! Please God let him be OK!" Her phone begins to ring and the call immediately ends. Anna picks up her phone and sees a missed call from Nick's phone.

Anna looks at her phone in anger. "Maybe Luis called me by mistake or he's so pissed that he ended the call before I could answer. I know he's pissed about Nick and I being together, but at this point, I don't give a fuck what Luis thinks! He didn't like me when I was dating Sam and I'm sure he hates me now. Well, fuck him! Fucking asshole! No one tells me who I can and can't be with!" Anna shouts as she defiantly presses the Redial button on her phone.

Luis gets into his car and places Nick's gym bag into the passenger seat. He leans back in the driver's seat and sighs. "I don't believe this shit! First Sam, now Nick. Is this bitch purposely going after my boys? It's her fault that Sam is dead. This whole 'love triangle' shit caused two deaths already! She's no good! Anna is a selfish, gold-digging slut that's just going to hurt Nick too. I can't think about that now. Nick is in the hospital. My boy is there are and I need to be there for him!" Luis thought. He starts the car and leaves the arena.

Luis looks at the road ahead of him as he drives towards the hospital. "Where the fuck is River Road? Damn GPS is useless, especially when these geniuses don't put signs up to identify the streets!" he thought. Nick's phone rings from the gym bag that is in the passenger seat. Luis grunts as he hears the phone ring and pulls the car over to the side of the road. He places the car in Park and reaches for the phone. Luis sees Anna's picture and name on the screen and growls. He hesitantly presses the Answer button and places the phone next to his ear and rolls his eyes as he hears Anna's voice.

Luis resists the urge to end the call as Anna speaks. "What does this bitch want now?" he thought. "Luis, it's Anna. We need to talk," Anna says. Luis unbuckles his seatbelt and exits the car so he can stretch. Luis stretches his arms and places the phone back to his ear. "What is it? I'm on the way to the hospital to see Nick!" he says loudly. Anna exhales and says, "Luis, I don't care if you like me or not. Right now all I care about is Nick. We both love Nick and want him to be OK. Any problems you have with me or Nick can wait."

Luis holds back a tear and says, "Anna, it's because of you one of my boys is gone! I'm not having a repeat of that! Yes, we will talk about this later, but now Nick is more important. I'll call you later and give you an update about Nick." Anna says, "OK" as the call is ended. She turns her head to crack her neck and places the phone on to the coffee table. Anna exhales and says, "I hope Nick is OK" and leans back so her head rests on the cushion from the couch. An image of Nick being carried away on a stretcher enters Anna's mind and she says, "Please be OK" as she falls asleep.

The bell rings signaling the start of the fight. Flashes of light enter Nick's field of vision from the cameras taking pictures. Nick is confused and has no idea who he is fighting. He looks across the octagon and sees Sam standing in the opposite corner. Sam's face and body are covered in blood and a small hole is protruding from the left side of his head.

Nick looks at his corner to talk to Luis and he is not there. He looks at Sam and Sam snarls. Sam looks at Nick and says, "If you think what I did to Thompson was bad, imagine what I'm going to do to you! You fucking scumbag! On the day of my funeral! You couldn't even wait for them to bury me! You're a dead man, brother!" Before Nick can reply, Sam advances towards him and attacks. Sam punches Nick and Nick collapses. As Nick falls to the canvas, Sam shouts, "I loved you man! Now you can go fuck yourself!"

Nick wakes up in a cold sweat from his bed and can barely breathe. He can feel the tubes that are up his nose and in this arms as he looks around the room. The clock on the wall says 6 am and the room is dark. "I must have passed out and I'm in the hospital. I can't breathe with these tubes in my nose!" he thought and removes the tubes from his nose.

Nick leans back on the bed and sighs. He says, "What a dream! I feel like Sam is haunting me or punishing me for seeing Anna. Thinking about Anna almost cost me the fight and I'm now in the hospital. I feel so guilty for what I did. I love Anna, but I can't live with this guilt. It's too much of a burden to bear" he thought.

The lights turn on and Luis enters the room. Nick smiles when he sees Luis and Luis walks over to the bed. Luis pulls up a chair next to Nick's bed and slowly sits down. Nick looks at Luis and sees the pain in Luis' face. He says, "Luis, thanks for being there for me. I feel better now. I think I'm going to be OK." Luis turns his head to hide his tears and wipes them away.

Luis turns to Nick and he tries not to cry. Seeing Nick in his current state saddens Luis. He says, "Kid, you really scared me tonight. In the octagon and after the fight. I'm happy to hear that you feel better, I really do, but I can't stop thinking about what happened earlier." Nick asks, "What are you talking about Luis? OK, I didn't have a great fight and I passed out, but you know me. I'll be OK." "It's not that Nick, I don't know how to sugar coat this, so I'm just going to say it. Are you and Anna dating? Are you sleeping with the woman that got Sam killed? The woman that is responsible for Sam's death?" Luis asks.

Nick is shocked by Luis' questions and cannot speak. Luis becomes enraged and yells, "¡Diga me pendejo! ¿Está con Anna? ¿Sí o no? Are you fucking Anna? Yes or no!" Nick lowers his head in shame and a single tear rolls down his cheek. Luis looks at Nick in disgust and says, "I can't believe you would do this to your brother! You and Sam grew up together! He brought you into my gym and helped you become the man that you are today! How can you do this?"

Nick is speechless as Luis yells at him. He avoids looking at Luis and keeps his head down in shame. Luis looks at Nick and says, "You let a piece of pussy cloud your thinking and betray the memory of Sam! I'm disgusted with you and that fucking cunt whore! She's the reason why Sam is dead!" Luis turns red with anger from yelling at Nick. He gets up from the chair and walks away from Nick.

Nick clenches his fists in anger at sits up. He looks at Luis and angrily says, "Luis, you better watch what you say about Anna. If I didn't love you like my father, I'd get out of this bed and kick your ass!" Luis turns around, runs towards Nick and slaps him in the face. A large, red hand print is left on Nick's face. Luis shouts, "¡Puto cabrón! You got some balls! I'm done with you! Don't ever come back to the dojo! I'm no longer your trainer and manager! You chose pussy over the people that care about you!" Luis starts to cry and pushes Nick's hand away as Nick reaches towards him. "I'm ashamed of you!" he shouts and storms out of the room.

Nick is speechless as Luis storms out of the room. His eyes water and tears roll down Nick's face. "I don't believe this shit! Luis didn't even give me a chance to speak! I know he's upset, but to just slap me like that and storm out! What the fuck?" he thought. Nick sobs and shouts, "I'm sorry! I'm so sorry!" and buries his face in his hands so no one can hear him cry.

Nick cries for several minutes until his phone rings. He turns towards the phone and sees Anna's picture on the screen. Nick wipes away his tears and reaches for the phone. His face and jaw sting from Luis' slap. "I forgot how hard Luis can hit. If he punched me, I'd probably be knocked out or worse" Nick thought. He presses the Answer button on the phone and hears Anna's voice.

Anna waits patiently as Nick's phone rings. "Please let Nick answer. I don't want to talk to Luis any more" she thought. She hears the call being answered and asks, "Nick? Nick? Is that you? Are you OK?" Nick pauses for a moment to calm himself and says, "No honey, I'm not good at all. I passed out after the fight, woke up with tubes in my nose and arms and Luis just quit on me. I'm not OK at all."

Anna is shocked by Nick's comments. Anna sighs and says, "Luis is really pissed at us being together. Well honey, if he can't accept the fact that we're together, tough shit. He doesn't tell us what to do and you're old enough to make your own decisions."

Tears begin to stream from Nick's eyes as he says, "Anna, you're wrong. We're wrong. I just lost the man that was like a father to me because of you. Luis saved my life! I would be in prison or dead if Luis didn't take me in after Sam brought me to his gym! I can't do this anymore!"

Anna is shocked by Nick's comments. Her hand starts to shake and she begins to cry while Nick speaks. She thought, "Please God, let this be a bad dream. I can't lose Nick! Please, not again!" Anna fearfully asks Nick, "Does this mean that you're breaking up with me? Nick, I love you! Please don't do this to me!" Anna pleads. Nick tearfully says, "I'm sorry Anna, I can't do this" and ends the call.

IV Old Friends

The phone rings loudly as it sits on the bedside table, disturbing Anna's sleep. Anna tosses and turns on her bed and opens her eyes from the sound of the phone. She groggily reaches for the phone and sees Jane's picture on the screen. Anna chuckles when she sees an image of Jane bent over, lifting her skirt exposing her buttocks and the phrase "Kiss my ass!" written in lipstick on her left cheek. "That Jane is too much sometimes" Anna thought as she presses the Answer button.

Jane eagerly waits for Anna to answer call. "Anna just hasn't been the same since Nick dumped her. I've never seen her like this. Come on Anna, answer the phone!" she thought. Anna answers the call and Jane smiles. "Anna! Anna! Wake your ass up! It's one o'clock in the afternoon! Get up! I'm not hanging up until you get up!" Jane says.

Anna sits up on the bed and yawns. She says, "Jane, what's the point? It's like I'm being punished for something I did. I lose every man that I care about. Paul is dead. Sam is dead. Nick dumped me. I'm too old for this shit!" Jane says, "Anna, you can't let this get to you like this. It's been a month since Nick left and all you've done is stay home. You haven't left your house, you don't call anyone or return phone calls, shit I'm lucky you answered my call! You can't let Nick have this effect on you. Anna, you are a strong woman who's been through a lot and we all care about you. Now stop this shit, get out of that fucking bed and get ready for tonight!" Jane says.

Anna is confused by Jane's last statement. She asks, "Who do you mean, 'Get ready for tonight?' What's happening tonight?" Jane answers, "We're taking you out tonight. We are not going to let you stay home alone, crying over some boy with daddy issues. If Nick can't stand up to Luis and wants to be with his 'daddy,' fuck him! You're getting back out there are going to enjoy life!" Anna yawns and says, "Jane, I appreciate it, but I'm not up to it. Maybe another time." After Anna finishes her sentence, the doorbell rings.

Anna gets out of the bed and puts on her robe. She says, "Jane, hold on a second, someone's at the door." Anna walks down the stairs, unlocks the door and opens it, surprised at who is standing there. Jane stands in front of Anna with a wide smile and says, "Gotcha!" Anna smiles and says, "You win again."

Jane enters the house as Anna holds open the door. Jane jokingly says, "I always do" as she enters the house and slaps Anna on the buttocks. Anna shouts, "Ow! That hurt! Dammit Jane!" Jane enters the house and says, "Damn girl! Open some windows! You need some fresh air in here! It smells like someone died in here! Let's open up the blinds and get some light in here! This place needs some life in it!"

Anna complies and opens the windows in the living room. Jane starts picking up empty pizza boxes, frozen dinners, empty bags of potato chips and bottles of wine from the floor. "Anna, this place is a mess! You'd think a single guy lived here, not a girl! I can't believe you let yourself go like this! Well, that shit changes today!" Jane says. Anna nods her head and says, "Thanks Jane, I needed that. I guess a swift kick to the ass helps once in a while."

Jane continues to clean up and smiles. She says, "You know I love you Anna. I don't want to see my girl down like this. You shut all of us out. When was the last time you spoke to your mother or any of us? You need to clear your head and move on. So go freshen yourself up and I'll finish up over here then go upstairs OK?" Anna says, "OK. I'll take a shower and freshen up." Jane says, "There you go! That's what I want to hear!"

Anna slowly walks up the stairs and goes into her bedroom. She takes off her robe leaving her completely nude. Anna looks at herself in the full-length mirror on the wall and is saddened by what she sees. Black circles surround her eyes from all of the sleepless, tearful nights since Nick broke up with her. Her face looks like she aged 5 years during the past month. New wrinkles are now appearing on her forehead and hands. Her stomach is not as toned as it used to be. Anna's buttocks is beginning to lose its curves, her arms are not has toned as they used to be and her breasts are slightly drooping from lack of exercise.

Anna turns away from the mirror in disgust. "I can't believe I let myself go like this! Jane is right, I can't let Nick have this effect on me. He hasn't called, texted or emailed me since that night. He doesn't return any of my calls and when I stopped by the dojo to try to speak to him in person, Luis had one of his dickhead goons prevent me from seeing Nick. Nick doesn't even go to his apartment since he's in training for his next fight" she thought. Anna goes into the bathroom and turns on the shower.

The water from the showerhead hits Anna's body as she enters the shower and she immediately jumps out. "Damn that's cold! I forgot that the knob for the hot water is broken. What a pain in the ass!" she thought. Anna firmly grips the knob labeled "Hot" and turns it until the water warms up. She extends her arm under the water until it reaches the temperature that Anna feels comfortable bathing with. Anna can hear Jane speaking to Susan downstairs as the rest of her friends have arrived. "Anna will be OK Susan. She just needs to get out and have some fun. A change of scenery, surrounded by friends will help her clear her mind" Jane says.

Anna smiles and stands under the showerhead as the water cascades down her body. She leans her head back and an image of Nick enters her mind. Nick is standing by the bathroom sink as Anna is rinsing soap off of her body. He is completely naked and breathing heavily from the thirty minutes they spent together in the bedroom. Anna smiles at first, then shakes her head saying, "No! Fuck that! Why should I think about that asshole when he dumped me? I thought he loved me! Shit!" Anna begins to cry and strikes the shower wall. She sits on the shower floor and sobs as the water begins to turn cold.

Jane looks up the stairs and is concerned. She turns to Susan and says, "What is taking Anna so long? She's been up there for a while." Susan looks at Miriam and Jane and says, "Maybe we should go up there and check. Let's make sure she's OK." They all nod in agreement and go up the stairs. Anna is curled into a fetal position on the shower floor sobbing loudly. "It's not fair! Why me? Why do I lose every man I love? What did I do to deserve this?"

Jane, Susan and Miriam go into the bathroom and pick Anna up from the floor. Miriam turns off the shower as Jane and Susan wrap a towel around Anna's wet body. They lead Anna into the bedroom and she sits on the bed. Anna lowers her head to avoid any eye contact with them as she weeps. Jane looks at Anna and says, "We're here for you Anna. You are not alone. We love you and care about you. You are our sister and we're here for you."

Jane, Miriam and Susan are all saddened by Anna's cries. Jane walks over to Anna and sits next to her on the bed. She holds Anna close to her and says, "We're here for you sweetie. We're here for you. We all love you. Forget about Nick. Sam is gone. It's time for you to live your life." Anna looks at Jane and says, "It's so hard Jane. You don't understand. Sam was killed by Paul and Nick almost dies from his fight and basically chose Luis over me. I feel like a toy that gets played with a couple of times then thrown to the side and forgotten about."

Jane and Miriam console Anna as Susan watches. Susan folds her arms and taps her foot. "I'm so sick of this shit!" she thought. Susan is angered by Anna's comments and says, "Anna, stop this shit! I think I speak for all of us when I say that we've heard enough about Sam and Nick! This self-pity, this crying shit has to stop! Stop feeling sorry for yourself, get dressed and get the fuck out of this house! We are going out and you're coming with us! Now let's go!" Anna, Jane and Miriam are shocked by Susan's comments. Anna smiles and says, "Yes sir!" and they all laugh.

Anna sits up from the bed and dries herself. Jane goes into Anna's closet and picks out a blue dress with matching shoes for Anna to wear. Susan leads Anna to the vanity desk and begins to apply makeup on her face. "Maybe I should have a breakdown more often, this is like being at a spa" Anna jokingly says. Jane, Miriam and Susan chuckle and Miriam says, "Don't get used to it bitch, next time you pay" and playfully smacks Anna on her buttocks. Anna sits still as Susan applies concealer and mascara to her face. "See Anna, all you needed was a little touch-up and now you look amazing. Look" Susan says.

Anna looks at herself in the mirror and smiles. She studies herself in the mirror and thought, "Wow! Susan did a great job! I look 10 years younger!" All of the imperfections that Anna noticed earlier are now gone. Susan looks at Anna and says, "Now you're back to normal." Anna hugs Susan and says, "Thanks Susie! I feel and look a whole lot better. Can you give me a minute to finish up and I'll meet you downstairs?" Jane, Miriam and Susan go downstairs together to the living room.

Anna goes into her dresser drawer and takes out a pink bra and thong. She slides her legs into the thong and thought, "I hope this still fits" and puts it on, followed by the bra. Anna stands in front of the full-length mirror and smiles. "What a difference! Earlier I looked horrible. Now I look and feel great! I can't wait to get out of here!" she thought. Anna puts on her dress and goes downstairs, holding her shoes in her hand.

Jane, Miriam and Susan all wait for Anna downstairs. When Anna appears, they begin to applaud and cheer. Anna blushes as she walks down the stairs and smiles. "You girls are too much!

Thanks!" she says. Jane says, "You look like a million bucks! Let's go out of here you sexy bitch!" Anna smiles and says, "OK, let's get out of here" and they all leave the house, ready for a night of fun.

V Small World

Anna, Jane, Miriam and Susan enter Jane's car. Anna asks, "Where are we going Jane?" Jane starts the car and says, "We're going to this new club that opened last week. It's not too far from here. When I heard about it, I knew we had to go." Anna smiles and says, "OK, that sounds good." Jane leaves Anna's house and gets on to the highway when Anna's phone rings. Anna thought, "Who could that be? I'm not expecting a call from anyone" and opens her purse to retrieve her phone.

Anna looks at her phone and sees Nick's picture and name displayed on the screen. A rush of excitement fills Anna's body as she reaches for her phone. Anna says, "Girls, you're not going to believe who's calling me!" and shows the phone to them. Jane, Miriam and Susan look at each other in disbelief. Miriam says, "I'd answer and tell Nick to 'go fuck himself' and hang up." Susan says, "I agree. After the way he treated you, I'm surprised you haven't blocked his calls."

Anna presses the Answer button on her phone and eagerly places it next to her ear. Jane whispers, "Put him on speaker! Let's see what excuse he has for treating you like shit!" Anna complies and presses the Speaker button on her phone so everyone can hear Nick speak. "Anna. Are you there? Look, I just wanted to call you and apologize for what I did. You understand what we were doing was wrong, but I realized that I made a mistake. I made a huge mistake and I want to be back with you. Anna, I love you very much and can't imagine a life without you" he says.

Anna fights back a tear and leans in her seat. She exhales and says, "Nick, you're too late. You treated me like shit and let Luis bully you into leaving me. Now you want me back? Why? You love me? You miss me? You miss fucking me? Well fuck you!" Nick can be heard clearing his throat and says, "Anna please, please forgive me. I never meant to hurt you. I do love you. Being away from you made me realize how I really felt about you and how special you are to me."

Anna listens to Nick speak and becomes upset. "Why couldn't he say this shit before? Why did Nick wait so fucking long to call me? I bet he tried being with someone else and can't stop thinking about me." She thought. Anna interrupts Nick and says, "Blah, blah, blah. I'm sick of hearing this shit! I go through the same shit with all of the men in my life and I've had enough. Nick, I wish you all the best, but I can't...I won't go back to you. It's over!" and ends the call.

As Anna speaks, Jane, Miriam and Susan nod their heads in agreement. They all cheer and Anna tries not to chuckle. An image of Nick enters Anna's mind and he begins to fade away as Anna speaks. When Anna shouts, "It's over!" Nick's image completely disappears from her mind.

Anna returns her attention back to Jane so she can hear what she's saying. Jane says, "It's about time! You needed to do that. Now you can really move on and take charge of your life. You don't need Nick or any other man to validate who you are!" Anna places her phone back into her purse and turns her head away from everyone as a single tear rolls down her cheek.

Jane slows the car down as she approaches the club. Anna looks at the entrance of the club and is mesmerized by the line of people waiting to enter the club and the sound of music coming from the club. Jane hands her keys to the valet and they all exit the car.

As Anna exits the car, she looks at the line of people. People ranging in age from their early 20's to their late 30's wait on the line. Everyone is dressed in the latest fashions, smelling of cologne and perfume as they eagerly wait to enter the club. Anna looks down the line and sees a familiar face in the line. Anna is in shock and quickly closes and opens her eyes to ensure that she is not imagining what she sees.

Standing in line is a short, blond-haired girl. Anna thought, "She looks like the one that was with Paul!" Anna vividly remembers that day as it plays back in her mind. She quietly goes up the stairs to her bedroom and sees a blond woman on top of Paul. His penis is in her mouth and her legs are spread open with his head buried between them. Anna remembers the shock and sadness she felt when she witnessed Paul cheating on her.

Anna begins to turn red with anger as she stares at the girl. The image of Paul with that girl will not go away. Jane sees Anna staring at the girl in the line and asks, "Anna, what's going on? Why are you staring at that girl? Do you know her?" Anna's hands turns into fists as she says, "That's the little whore that I caught sucking Paul's dick! That fucking bitch is here! She's probably looking for another man to seduce and breakup another marriage!"

Jane, Miriam and Susan physically restrain Anna. They lead her away from the club entrance as Anna resists. Jane looks at Anna and says, "Anna, calm down! First of all, are you sure it's her? Second, if it is her, is she worth going to jail for? If you beat the shit out of her here, you will get arrested." Anna shouts, "I don't care! That little whore stole my husband from me and started this whole mess!" and starts to cry.

Anna's friends try to console her as she weeps. Miriam says, "Anna we don't have to go here. We can go someplace else. You don't need to be reminded about the past. The last thing we want is for you to go to jail over some skank. We want you to have a good time." "No, I'm OK. We're here already. Let's just go in and I won't even look in her direction" Anna says. Jane, Miriam and Susan reluctantly agree and they all return to the club entrance.

Anna calms herself as they approach the club. They are greeted by a very large man standing guard at the velvet rope. Jane approaches him and he smiles. The bouncer opens the velvet rope for them and Jane says, "Thanks Harold." He says, "Any time Jane. You ladies enjoy yourselves" as they enter the club. Anna asks Jane, "How do you know him? He's huge!"

Jane leads her friends into the club and blows a kiss at the bouncer. He smiles and says, "Call me." Jane returns her attention to her friends and says, "That's Harold. He was a body builder during the 70's and 80's. He won every title except Mr. Olympia. We went out a few times, but it didn't work out. He's better just being a friend with benefits. Before you perverts ask, yes...he's big everywhere." Anna, Miriam and Susan all laugh and the walk towards the dance floor.

Music is being played very loudly in the background as Jane leads the group to a table with a "Reserved" sign on it. Jane invites them all to sit and a server brings a bottle of champagne to the table. "Compliments of the house" the server says as she pours the champagne into their glasses. Anna looks around the club and is impressed. "This place is great! I really like the way it's setup and the music is really good. I can see why people are lined up to get in here. I'm glad the girls did this for me. Now that Nick is out of my life, I can focus more on my life" she thought.

Anna raises her glass to her lips and sees Lisa on the dance floor. A surge of anger fills her body and she tries to calm down. An image of Lisa lying on top of Paul enters Anna's mind and she becomes enraged. Anna gulps down her drink and quickly refills her glass. Susan notices how Anna is staring at Lisa and asks, "Anna, is everything OK?" Anna says, "I'm fine Susan...just fine" as she drinks her second glass of champagne.

As the night passes on, Anna continues to drink champagne and any other drink that is placed in front of her. She continues to focus on Lisa's whereabouts and notices that Lisa is heading towards the Ladies room. Anna puts down her drink and says, "Excuse me girls, I have to go to the bathroom." Miriam says, "I'll go with you" and Anna quickly says, "No, I'm OK. I really have to go. I'll be back soon."

Anna gets up from the table and staggers to the Ladies room. Anna looks directly at the door to the Ladies Room so she can focus. She stares at the sign on the door and pauses. "Now's my chance! I finally get to confront this little bitch!" she thought. Anna places her hand on the door to push it open and pauses. She exhales and slowly pushes open the door.

Lisa is standing in front of the mirror adjusting her dress. Anna leans against the wall and stares at Lisa. Lisa looks into the mirror and smiles. She turns around and looks at Anna. Lisa says, "I was wondering when you were going to say something to me. I saw you looking at me earlier. I don't usually hook up with women, but you're looking fine mamí. I'd love to hook up with you."

Anna is shocked by Lisa's comments and is speechless. "What the fuck? I don't believe this! This little whore is hitting on me!" Anna thought. Lisa walks up to Anna and puts her hand on the wall. Anna is frozen in shock as Lisa approaches her. Lisa leans towards Anna and whispers, "Do you think I'm sexy? Do I make you nervous? Well, you don't have to be" and kisses Anna on the lips.

Anna is frozen in shock and confusion. "What the fuck is going on here? I wanted to confront this bitch and she thinks I want to fuck her! I don't believe this!" she thought. Lisa steps back from Anna and smiles. "Is this the first time you've been kissed by a girl? Don't worry, it's OK to be a little scared. I like older lovers, especially women that have never been with another woman" Lisa says.

Anna is in a state of disbelief as Lisa speaks. Lisa kisses Anna again while cupping Anna's left breast. Anna allows Lisa to cup her breast and opens her mouth so Lisa can insert her tongue into her mouth. "I can't believe I'm doing this! Why am I so turned on by this? She's so small and delicate, but she's also dominant at the same time. Is this what attracted Paul to her? This is too much!" Anna thought.

Anna and Lisa kiss for several minutes. Lisa moves closer to Anna and places her hands on Anna's body. She rubs Anna's buttocks while Anna wraps her arms around Lisa's body. Anna pauses and pushes Lisa back and Lisa is shocked. "What's wrong? Are you having second thoughts? Don't tell me you're one of those people that like to 'experiment,' one of those women that can't admit that they like women!" Anna starts to cry and says, "No, it's not that! I know who you are! You slept with my husband! You slept with Paul!"

Lisa steps back from Anna in shock. She adjusts her dress, pulling it down and composes herself. She looks at Anna and says, "Let me get this right. You're Paul's wife and you came in here to seduce me, confront me or both? What's going on here?" Anna wipes her mouth and adjusts her dress. She looks at Lisa and says, "I wanted to confront you. You have no idea what you did to me! Do you know that Paul is dead?"

Lisa moves away from Anna and is in shock. Lisa starts to sob and Anna begins to sob as well. Lisa tearfully says, "I'm so sorry. I heard something about Paul being dead, but I couldn't believe it. I stopped talking to Paul after I last saw him and got a job elsewhere, so I didn't know. When his picture was on the news, I was in shock. I couldn't believe...I wouldn't believe that Paul was capable of killing someone. Anna, I didn't know that Paul was that crazy. I'm so sorry for what I did to you."

Anna tries to fight back her tears and leans on the wall in grief. Lisa walks over to Anna and holds her to comfort her. Anna leans her head against Lisa's breasts and cries. Lisa and Anna cry for several minutes and stop to look at each other. "This is so weird" Lisa says and Anna nods in agreement. They separate from each other and Anna adjusts her dress while Lisa applies lipstick to her lips.

Anna stops crying as she composes herself. She checks her lips and sees remnants of Lisa's purple lipstick on her mouth. A faint grin appears on Anna's lips as she looks at the purple smears on her fingers. "As much as I want to deny it, I liked the way Lisa kisses. Her lips are so soft and her body felt nice next to mine. I can see why Paul was with her. Stop thinking about that Anna! She broke up your marriage!" she thought.

Anna goes over to the sink and begins to wash off the lipstick. Lisa asks, "Are you OK now? Are WE OK now? I really don't want..." Anna interrupts Lisa, raising her index finger and says, "We have a lot to talk about. Give me your phone number and we'll make arrangements to meet." Lisa says, "OK, let's do that" and takes her phone out of her purse. Anna says, "My number is 818-555-6270." Lisa dials Anna's phone number and Anna's phone rings, displaying Lisa's phone number. Anna looks at her phone, then at Lisa and says, "I'll call you later, OK?" Lisa nods her head and Anna leaves the room.

Anna returns to the table and her friends all look at Anna with concern. "What took you so long? We saw you follow that girl into the bathroom. Did you beat her up? What happened? Do you want Harold to kick her out of here?" Jane asks. Anna sits down and reaches for a glass of champagne. Her hand shakes nervously as she reaches for the glass. Anna exhales and breathes slowly so she can calm herself. She drinks the champagne and can taste Lisa's lipstick on her lips.

An image of Lisa kissing her, touching her breast enters Anna's mind. "I can't believe Lisa kissed me! She's a very daring person! I guess that's what attracted Paul to her. It felt weird, but felt good at the same time. I've been hit on by women before, but never kissed, I mean never been kissed by another woman. Her soft lips, gentle touch kind of turned me on. Wait a minute! What am I thinking? Lisa stole Paul from me! Then again, Paul went psycho and tried to kill me and killed Sam. This is so fucking confusing and frustrating! I should have just slapped Lisa and be done with it. I'll call her and just meet with her so I can put all of this behind me" she thought. Anna finishes her drink and says, "Everything's fine" and smiles.

VI We Meet Again...

"I'm glad you called. This is so weird that we're meeting like this. I never thought that we would be sitting here like this. It's so odd" Lisa says. Anna avoids looking at Lisa as she stares at her coffee. Her heart races as Lisa speaks. Anna stirs her coffee with her spoon, takes it out of the cup, placing it on a napkin and drinks her coffee. Anna places the cup on to the saucer, looks at Lisa and says, "Yes, this is odd. How many woman can say they're having coffee with the woman they caught with their husbands?" Lisa looks away from Anna in shame.

Anna extends her arm and touches Lisa's hand so she can look at her. "You understand where I'm coming from? How would you feel if someone did that to you? I don't think you'd be as civil as I am" Anna says. Lisa nods her head an agreement and exhales. Anna looks at Lisa in the eye and asks, "Why? Why did you sleep with my husband? Why not someone else? You can have any man you want. What would make you do that?"

Lisa removes her hand from the table and slowly drinks her coffee. She lowers her cup and sighs. Anna can see how nervous Lisa is and stops looking directly at Lisa so she can calm herself. Lisa finally calms herself and looks at Anna. She exhales and says, "I met Paul at work. I'm not going to lie to you. You've been through a lot and the least I can do is tell you the truth."

Anna drinks her coffee as Lisa speaks. She avoids eye contact with Lisa so she can focus on what Lisa is saying. Lisa says, "When I first saw Paul, I was instantly attracted to him. He was handsome, intelligent, confident and powerful. He was a man among men. Seeing him in the office, how he carried himself, how he dominated that company, seeing everyone respect and fear him at the same time, it turned me on."

Anna looks at Lisa and then looks away. "Paul had the same effect on me" she thought. Lisa continues and says, "When I started working with Paul, I became even more attracted to him. Seeing how passionate Paul was at his job, how intense he can be made me want him more and more. Just so you know, I pursued him. I wanted him and did what I had to do to get him. Paul was a passionate lover. He surprised me. I thought that since he was older than me, he would not be as good as he was. I was wrong. Paul satisfied me in every way except one. He was never really mine. Even with all of the problems you both had, his heart still belonged to you."

Lisa starts to sob and Anna holds Lisa's hand again to calm her down. Anna can feel Lisa's hand tremble and feels sympathy for her. She rubs Lisa's hand until Lisa stops trembling. "I can't believe how emotional Lisa is becoming! It's as if SHE was married to Paul!" Anna thought. Tears flow from Lisa's eyes and Anna is saddened at the sight of Lisa's tears. "She really loved Paul! All this time I thought that Lisa was just a little gold-digging slut that just wanted a 'sugar daddy' but she really loved Paul! She loved Paul just as much as I did! Damn you Paul!" Anna thought.

Lisa wipes away her tears and composes herself. Anna beckons a server to the table and asks Lisa, "Do you want another coffee or something else to drink?" Lisa whispers, "Another coffee" and Anna orders two coffees. Lisa clears her throat and places the napkin she used to wipe her tears back on to the table. The server leaves and Lisa says, "Thank you. Anna, I have never felt like I had for any man until I met Paul. I loved him! Even after you caught us and he dumped me, I still loved him! I tried to get him back, I really tried, but he always loved you! He even screamed your name after he came the last time I saw him. After that, I knew that he will never be mine. He really did love you Anna."

Anna begins to weep from guilt. She feels guilty about that night Sam came to her house. An image of Sam enters her mind as he carries Anna up to her bedroom while Paul was unconscious on the floor. Sam throws Anna on to the bed and forces Anna to open her mouth. He inserts his penis into her mouth and Anna remembers how salty and sweaty it was. Anna almost gagged from the taste of Sam's penis, but didn't fearing what Sam would do to her.

Anna tries to fight her tears as Lisa waits for a reply. She remembers how Paul struggled to climb the stairs and the look on his face when he entered the bedroom. Anna was on top of Sam, riding his penis shouting, "Fuck me!" "Paul tried to defend me, save me from Sam, but I chose Sam over him! Who knows what would have happened if I chose differently? They would both be alive. I would be with Sam!" she thought.

Tears flow from Anna's eyes and Lisa begins to cry. She sees Anna in tears and reaches over to console her. "We both loved Paul. I guess he had that effect on both of us. I haven't seen anyone else since Paul was at my apartment and I think it's time I moved on" Lisa says. Anna wipes away her tears and says, "Yes, Paul definitely had an effect on both of us. I've been going in circles since the day that Paul shot Sam and I. I even slept with Sam's friend. He reminded me so much about Sam and was so nice...I didn't think. Now I have no one in my life."

Anna starts to cry again and Lisa leans towards her. Lisa kisses Anna on the cheek, making Anna feel uneasy. "You'll be OK Anna. I'll be OK. We'll be OK. We don't need a man to validate ourselves. We don't need a man to make us feel wanted. We don't need a man to feel needed. All we need is each other" Lisa says and kisses Anna on the cheek, very close to her lips.

Anna is confused by Lisa's gesture. She looks at Lisa and asks, "Are you kissing me to console me or something else?" Lisa blushes and says, "Both. To be honest with you Anna, before you told me who you were, I was attracted to you. Like I said at the club, I don't normally do this, but you do it for me. When we kissed, it made me wet and I wanted more."

Anna is speechless and has no idea how to respond. "This is so fucking weird! We're both here talking about my dead husband and the woman that seduced him now wants to seduce me! As strange as that sounds, I'm actually excited about this. Lisa is very beautiful and she made me curious about being with her. I've never been with a woman" she thought.

Lisa moves closer to Anna. She holds Anna's hand and places small kisses on Anna's neck. Anna's body tenses up from Lisa's gentle kisses and she moves closer to Lisa. Anna tries to resist Lisa's advances but fails. "I can't resist, I must have her!" Anna thought. She says, "We're lucky we're in a dark booth so no one can see us" and holds Lisa by her head, kissing her on the lips.

Lisa and Anna kiss passionately for several minutes. The server arrives as they are kissing and interrupt them. "Excuse me ladies, I'm sorry for the delay, but here are your coffees" the server says. The server tries to hide his smile as he places the tray of cups on to the adjacent table. Anna and Lisa blush and say, "Thank you." The server places the coffee cups on to their table and leaves.

Anna and Lisa wait for the server to leave. Lisa turns to Anna and asks, "You want to get out of here and come back to my place?" Anna pauses and says, "Yes." Lisa smiles and kisses Anna again on the lips. Anna holds Lisa close to her so they can kiss passionately again. "She really knows how to kiss, even better than Paul and Sam" Anna thought.

Anna and Lisa continue to kiss passionately for several minutes. They stop kissing and Anna reaches for the check. Lisa puts her hand on top of Anna's hand and smiles. She says, "No, I'll get it" and winks. Anna smiles and removes her hand from the check. Lisa picks up the check and Anna says, "OK, I'll get the tip." Anna reaches into her purse and takes out a five dollar bill, placing it on to the table.

Anna and Lisa leave the table with a hurried excitement. Anna looks at Lisa's body as she walks ahead of her, examining every detail. "Lisa has a great body! Her legs, her ass, her breasts, all perfectly curved and symmetrical. Not too big, not too small, she's perfectly proportioned. She looks like a model. I can't believe I'm staring at her like this and I want her! I'm so conflicted! Should I stop now and not sleep with Lisa or should I satisfy my cravings and my curiosity by sleeping with Lisa? No! I want her! I want to feel her body next to mine! I want her to hold and kiss me until I'm wet" she thought.

Lisa pays the check and smiles at Anna. She blows a kiss at Anna, making Anna blush. They leave the café and Lisa says, "You can follow me. I'm not too far from here." Anna says, "OK" and they enter their cars. Lisa leaves the café first as Anna follows in her car. Anna's heart races in excitement as she follows Lisa's car.

Anna follows Lisa's car and is in disbelief. "This is really happening" Anna thought as she stops behind Lisa's car. They park in front of the building where Lisa lives and Anna pauses before exiting her car. "This is so odd and exciting! I know Susan experimented in college and told me she liked it, but I never thought I'd do this! OK Anna, it's now or never" she thought.

Lisa taps on Anna's window so she can roll it down. "You're not any having second thoughts are you?" Lisa asks. Anna says, "No, not really. Just thinking." Lisa smiles and says, "Come on. I'm on the first floor." Anna rolls her window up, turns the key in the ignition to turn off the car and exits. Lisa walks in front of Anna as they enter the building. They walk down the hallway that leads to Lisa's apartment.

Lisa reaches for her keys as she approaches her apartment. Anna grabs Lisa's hand and says, "I'm not sure I want to do this.

It just feels weird. You had an affair with Paul and now we're going to your place. It just feels wrong." Lisa looks at Anna and says, "I can't force you to do anything you don't want to do. All I can say is that I want you and there must be something about me that made you come here." Lisa kisses Anna on the lips and Anna places Lisa's hand on her left breast.

Anna and Lisa kiss passionately in front of Lisa's apartment for several minutes. Lisa stops kissing Anna and asks, "You still don't want to come in?" Anna jokingly says, "Shut up and open the door," playfully grabbing Lisa's buttocks. Lisa opens the door and immediately closes it after Anna enters the apartment. Anna starts to take off her blouse and Lisa says, "No, allow me."

Anna nervously stands still as Lisa touches her. She moves her hands away from her blouse and Lisa slowly unbuttons her blouse as she kisses Anna's neck. Lisa purposely takes her time unbuttoning Anna's blouse, savoring every moment. Anna's body trembles as Lisa kisses and licks her neck. Anna has never been as aroused as she feels now. "No one has ever made me feel like this! This feels so good! I'm so turned on now! She knows where to go and how to get me excited. Just take off my clothes already and make me wet!" Anna thought.

Lisa removes Anna's blouse and leads Anna to her bed. She continues to kiss Anna on the lips and neck. They enter Lisa's bedroom and Lisa removes Anna's bra, exposing her firm, erect nipples. Anna and Lisa lie on the bed, side by side. Lisa slides her body over Anna's and Anna jokingly says, "I see you like to be on top." Lisa smiles and says, "My bed, so I'm in control" and starts to take off Anna's skirt.

Anna stares at Lisa as she removes her clothes. "She is so beautiful!" Anna thought. Anna starts to lift up Lisa's dress and while doing so, it becomes entangled on Lisa's body. Anna and Lisa burst into laughter and Anna joking says, "Now you can't go anywhere." She helps untangle Lisa's dress so she can lift it off of her head. Anna stares at Lisa's body as she sits on top of her. She says, "You're so beautiful. I have never been with a woman before, but I want you. Take me!" Lisa smiles and says, "With pleasure."

Lisa lies on top of Anna and kisses her. She strokes Anna's hair with one hand and plays with Anna's pink lace thong with the other. Lisa caresses Anna's buttocks, slowly lowering Anna's thong. Anna holds Lisa's head so she can insert her tongue into Lisa's mouth. She uses her free hand to remove Lisa's bra. Anna fumbles with the hook on the back of Lisa's bra and becomes frustrated. "Damn hooks! It's like they make these bras child-proof!" Anna thought. Lisa sits up on Anna's body and says, "Let me get that." She reaches behind her back and removes her bra.

Anna stares at Lisa's breasts, admiring how firm and perky they are. Lisa smiles and starts to remove her panties while rubbing herself against Anna's body. Anna giggles and playfully slaps Lisa on her buttocks, leaving a red handprint on her left cheek. Lisa finishes removing her panties and begins to remove Anna's pink lace thong. Anna pulls Lisa close to her and kisses Lisa passionately, biting Lisa's lips and sucking on her neck. "If I knew being with a woman was this intense, I would have done this a long time ago!" Anna thought.

Lisa finishes removing Anna's thong and they are now completely naked. Lisa slowly rubs her leg against Anna's body, making Anna's body tense. The sensation Anna feels from Lisa's smooth skin arouses her. "Lisa's skin is so soft and smooth. I'm so used to rough, hairy skin from men, this is quite a change. This is relaxing and arousing at the same time. Oh my God Lisa, just fuck me already!" Anna thought.

Anna moves closer to Lisa as she continues to rub against Anna's body. The warmth of Lisa's body and breath excites Anna. "Take me! I want you now!" Anna shouts. Lisa starts to lick Anna's body slowly with her tongue starting with Anna's neck. Lisa licks Anna's neck and her body tenses up from the sensation and warmth of Lisa's tongue. Lisa fondles Anna's right breast with her hand and sucks on her left breast. "Suck my breast! Yes, just like that!" Anna shouts.

Lisa continues to suck on Anna's left breast and moves her hand slowly down Anna's body. Lisa starts to play with Anna's vagina, slowly rubbing the clitoris while Anna grinds her body against Lisa's body. Anna's body twists and turns in ecstasy as Lisa fondles her. Lisa whispers, "You want me to stop baby?" Anna whispers, "No, don't stop...ugh!" and Lisa continues to rub Anna's clitoris with her finger. "Tell me you want me" Lisa whispers as she gently bites on Anna's ear. Anna shouts, "I want you! I want you! Take me!"

Lisa smiles and places a second finger by Anna's clitoris, rubbing it faster. Anna spreads her legs wider so Lisa can access her vagina. Lisa starts to lick the center of Anna's stomach, slowly moving her tongue down towards Anna's vagina. She moves her tongue in different directions, making Anna squirm. "Oh my God! This feels so good! Keep going, keep going! Make me wet!" Anna arches her body in ecstasy as Lisa licks her body. "Holy shit! Keep going, keep going! Don't stop! Make this pussy yours!" Anna shouts.

Lisa pauses from licking Anna's body and smiles. She slowly moves her tongue around the exterior of Anna's vagina, licking every inch of it. Anna grabs on to the head board as Lisa licks her. "Oh my God she's good! She hasn't started eating my pussy yet and I'm ready to cum! I've never felt like this in my life! Stop teasing me and eat my pussy already!" Anna thought. Lisa can see every detail of Anna's vagina. "You have a beautiful pussy. I wonder if it tastes as good as it looks" Lisa says as she lowers her head between Anna's legs.

Lisa begins to lick Anna's vagina. She slowly moves her tongue across Anna's vagina, making Anna moan. Anna's body tenses some more and she tightens her grip on the head board. Anna's left leg starts to shake as Lisa inserts her tongue inside of Anna's vagina. She lifts her head and whispers, "You like this baby?" and Anna shouts, "Yes, keep going, don't stop! Eat my pussy! Make me wet!" Lisa smiles and says, "You're wish is my command" and lowers her head, inserting her tongue and index finger into Anna's vagina.

Lisa inserts and removes her tongue and finger first at a slow then a rapid pace as Anna moans in ecstasy. Lisa starts to feel Anna's warm, thick ejaculation on her finger while Anna shouts, "I'm cumming!" Lisa removes her finger and places her mouth on Anna's vagina. She licks and sucks on Anna's clitoris while Anna grabs the back of her head. Anna pushes Lisa's head closer to her vagina shouting, "Oh my God! This is so fucking good! Eat my pussy!"

Anna continues to scream and moan as Lisa licks and sucks on her vagina. Lisa begins to adjust her body so her neck doesn't tense up and become stiff. Anna looks at the curves of Lisa's buttocks as it is now up in the air. "Lisa's ass looks so good! I love how round and firm it is" Anna thought. She adjusts her body so she can touch Lisa's buttocks. Anna starts to fondle Lisa's buttocks and Lisa move her body sideways so Anna can reach her buttocks.

Anna massages Lisa's curvaceous buttocks and slowly moves her hand towards Lisa's vagina. Anna feels the exterior of Lisa's vagina and the warmth between her legs. She rubs her fingers against Lisa's inner thighs and thought, "Even her vagina is perfectly smooth! As much as I shave myself, I still have some stubble! Her skin is so smooth, just touching her turns me on!" Lisa's legs begin to tense as Anna slowly rubs her clitoris. Anna continues to rub Lisa's clitoris when Lisa says, "Stop teasing me and finger fuck me already!" Anna smiles and inserts her index finger inside of Lisa's vagina.

Lisa continues to lick Anna's vagina as Anna moans. Anna inserts her finger into Lisa's vagina and Lisa begins to moan. She continues to insert and remove her finger for several minutes. Lisa moves her body so her vagina is now on top of Anna's face and spreads her legs. Anna removes her finger from Lisa's vagina and hesitates. "I've never done this before. I've had this done to me so many times, so I'm pretty sure I'll do this right" Anna thought.

Anna places her hands on both sides of Lisa's vagina, spreading it open. She looks at Lisa's vagina and pauses. "I've gone this far so there's no turning back now" she thought. Anna begins to lick Lisa's vagina, slowly moving her tongue across the exterior and interior of it. Lisa starts to moan loudly as Anna licks her clitoris, wagging her tongue against it then inserting it deep into Lisa's vagina.

Anna continues to lick Lisa's vagina as Lisa shouts in ecstasy. "Her pussy is so wet! I can taste the cum from her pussy and I want more!" Anna thought. Anna tightens her grip on Lisa's buttocks and moves her head up and down Lisa's vagina. She licks every inch of Lisa's vagina until Lisa ejaculates. Lisa's warm, thick ejaculation squirts on to Anna's face as she also ejaculates on to Lisa's face. Lisa relaxes her legs and Anna loosens her grip on Lisa's buttocks.

Anna rests her head on Lisa's pillow and smiles. She stops arching her body as Lisa continues to lick her vagina. Lisa slowly lifts her leg, turning her body so she can now see Anna face-to-face. Lisa smiles and asks, "Did you like that? I hope you did. I really enjoyed eating your pussy." Anna looks at Lisa and notices that her mouth and chin are wet.

Lisa stares at Anna while she waits for a reply. "I hope she liked that. Anna made me cum really hard" Lisa thought. Anna quickly touches her face and realizes that her face is also wet. Anna smiles and blushes when Lisa points at her. Lisa chuckles and says, "I got you too! We're both squirters!" They both smile and burst into laughter.

Anna reaches up to hold Lisa by the head and kisses her passionately. Anna looks at Lisa and says, "I enjoyed every minute. I've never cum so hard in my life. You really turn me on" and kisses Lisa again. Anna fondles Lisa's breasts and kisses Lisa's neck. Lisa begins to cup Anna's breasts when Anna's phone rings. Lisa removes her hands from Anna's breasts and reaches for Anna's purse. "Thank you" Anna says as Lisa gives her the purse.

Anna looks at her phone and is shocked at who is calling her. She sees that Nick is calling her and frowns. "Of all of the worst timing to have! He calls now? What the hell? What does he want?" Anna thought. Lisa looks at Anna and asks, "Is that your boyfriend?" Anna blushes and says, "Yes, no...I mean NO. He dumped me a little while ago. It's a long story. I'll let it go to voicemail."

Anna's phone rings again and she sees that Nick is calling again. "If he's calling back and not leaving a voicemail, it may be important" Lisa says. Anna presses the Answer button on her phone and sighs. "Anna, thanks for picking up. Please don't hang up. I'm calling because I have some great news and I wanted to share this with you. I'm fighting for the championship! The guy that was supposed to fight next month was injured while training and I'm taking his place! This is so awesome!" Nick says.

Anna frowns as she listens to Nick on the phone. "I really don't want to talk to him now. I want to be with Lisa now and he's interrupting us!" Anna thought. She moves the phone away from her ear and makes a talking gesture with her hand, making Lisa giggle. Anna mouths the words, "Who gives a fuck?" and Lisa tries not to laugh. Lisa holds her two fingers to her mouth and sticks her tongue between them, making Anna smile.

Anna places the phone back to her ear. She sarcastically says, "Well, congratulations. I'm happy to hear that, but I'm a little busy now. I'll talk to you later." Nick hurriedly says, "Anna, I know you're still angry at me because of the way I treated you, but I'm really sorry. This is what we have talked about before. I'll win the title and we can both live together in the lap of luxury. I made a mistake Anna. I should have told Luis about us sooner. I should have stood up to him and never should have left you. I ask you...no...beg you, please give me a second chance. I love you." Lisa looks at Anna with a look of concern as Anna starts to cry.

Anna moves the phone away from her ear and wipes away her tears. Lisa moves closer to Anna and asks, "Do you want some privacy? I can go into the living room if you want." Anna nods her head and places the phone back to her ear. Lisa gets up from the bed, wraps a sheet around her body and leaves. She goes into the living room and sits on the couch. Lisa looks back as she walks towards the living room and she sees the sadness in Anna's expression.

Lisa looks at Anna and is concerned. "I hope this guy doesn't hurt Anna. I really like her and don't want to see her get hurt again. I've never been so attracted to someone like this in my life. I hope she doesn't go back to this guy" Lisa thought. She continues to look at Anna while Anna speaks. Lisa fights back a tear and whispers, "I hope he doesn't hurt her. I hope she doesn't go back to him."

Anna places the phone back to her ear and pauses. She says, "Nick, you caught me at a very awkward moment. You really hurt me when you dumped me. You broke my heart. I couldn't do anything. I didn't want to do anything. I didn't leave my house. I stayed in bed all day. That's what you did to me. Now after all of this time has passed, you want me to take you back and act like nothing ever happened?" Anna says.

Nick scratches his head and massages his neck before answering Anna. He exhales and says, "Anna, I don't know what else to say to you. I was an idiot, no I AM an idiot. You mean more to me than anyone else. You're caring, kind and make me happy. You made me realize that what we have is special and I fucked that up. Anna, all I'm asking for is a second chance. If I fuck up again, I won't bother you again."

Anna removes the phone from her ear, looks at herself then looks around the bedroom. She can see Lisa sitting on the couch wrapped in the bed sheet that they just made love on. Lisa looks at the living room floor as she waits for Anna. Anna notices the sad look on Lisa's face and frowns. She looks at herself as she lies nude in Lisa's bed. Anna's vagina is still throbbing from the intense orgasm that Lisa gave her. "What do I do? None of this was supposed to happen. I have a secret relationship with Nick, lose him, confront Lisa, kiss her, come over here and sleep with her! Jesus Christ, this is confusing! I still care about Nick and even though I just met Lisa, I really like her" she thought.

Anna places the phone back to her ear after looking at Lisa. Lisa looks at Anna and slides off of the couch and quietly walks over to the bedroom door. She stands in the doorway to listen to Anna's call. Anna says, "Nick, I still care about you. Everything was going great until you dumped me. I have a lot on my mind and I can't say 'yes' or 'no' now. I have to call you back OK?" Nick says, "OK Anna, I understand. I hope to hear from you soon" and ends the call. Anna places the phone next to her body and sees Lisa standing in the doorway.

Lisa looks at Anna in anger. Tears roll down Lisa's face as she stares at Anna. "I can't believe this! It's happening again! Why does this always happen to me?" Lisa thought. Anna is confused by Lisa's stare and asks, "What's wrong?" Lisa angrily says, "Why didn't you just say 'No'? Why did you tell him you'll call him back? You said he dumped you, so why would you even consider going back to him? I know we just met, but I thought that we really may have something! I don't just sleep around with anyone that I meet. I'm not some slut that just fucks whomever I want! I thought that we may have something here."

Anna is stunned by Lisa's reaction and is speechless. "I don't believe this! You're just as bad as Paul! You use me for your sexual pleasure then throw me to the side like an empty beer can! I can't believe I fell for this again! First Paul, now you! What was I thinking? Jesus!" Lisa shouts. Anna looks down at the bed to avoid eye contact with Lisa. Lisa bangs her fist against the bedroom door and shouts, "Get out! Get out of here now!"

Anna quickly gets out of Lisa's bed. She looks at Lisa and says, "I'm sorry. I didn't mean for this to happen. I didn't use you Lisa, I..." Lisa interrupts Anna and says, "I don't want to hear it! I'm not in the mood for your bullshit!" Anna reaches over to console Lisa and she pushes Anna's arm away. "Don't touch me! Just leave!" Lisa tearfully says. Anna quickly puts on her clothes and leaves Lisa's apartment. She walks down the hallway and exits the building.

Anna pauses before entering her car and sighs. "What just happened back there? One minute I'm having sex with Lisa, the next minute she's throwing me out of her apartment! Why did Nick have to call now? Why did I take his call? I could have ignored his call and I'd still be in there with Lisa. Damn! As much as I has to say it, I still care about Nick. He saved my life! I can't be angry at him because of the situation I put him in. We had sex on the day of Sam's funeral! I just had sex with the woman that had an affair with Paul!" Anna thought. She enters her car, places the key in the ignition and starts the car. Anna leans back into her seat and sighs. Anna's phone rings and she sees Nick's name displayed on the dashboard screen. She reaches over to press the green Answer button and says, "Nick, we need to talk..."

VII The Rebound

Anna drives away from Lisa's apartment as Nick patiently waits for her to speak. She can hear Nick breathing in the background over her car's speakers. The sound of Nick breathing makes Anna feel at ease. Nick waits in excitement as Anna exhales and says, "Nick, I don't know how to say this delicately so I'm just going to say it. I just left someone's apartment. You called me when I just slept with someone."

Nick is saddened and upset by Anna's statement. He mouths the words, "What the fuck?" Nick pauses and asks, "Anna, are you joking or are you being serious with me? Please tell me you're joking." As Nick waits for Anna's reply, he slams his fist into a pillow. "Fuck! I knew this was going to happen! Some mother fucker slept with Anna before I can win her back! Fuck! I don't know if I should even continue with this. If she won't talk to me now, I'm not going to continue with this" he thought.

Anna begins to chuckle and stops herself. "No, Nick. I'm not joking. Besides, what makes you think that I can't be with anyone else after you dumped me? You don't own or control me!" Anna shouts. Nick puts the phone on Mute so Anna can't hear him. "Fuck! I'm pouring my heart out to this bitch and she tells me she just fucked another man! Bitch!" he shouts. Nick exhales and says, "Nick, calm yourself down. Anna is right. You dumped her. She's no longer yours. Calm yourself." Nick presses the Mute button again so he can talk to Anna.

Nick calms himself so he can continue his conversation with Anna. He quickly says, "No, no, no! I didn't mean it like that. It's just that...it's shocking to hear someone you love say that she just slept with another man. How would you feel if I called you and said that I slept with another woman? I don't think you'd like that."

Anna smiles and tries not to laugh. She thought, "I can only imagine what he'll say when I tell that I slept with Lisa. He'll really be shocked." Nick waits for Anna's reply as he paces back and forth in his apartment. He sits on a large chair and exhales as Anna begins to speak. She says, "No, I don't think I'd like that, but I wouldn't care because we aren't together anymore. I am not yours and you don't own me."

Nick is angered by Anna's comment and starts to grind his teeth. Anna can hear a clicking sound in the background and asks, "What's that sound?" Nick stops grinding his teeth and says, "There must have been some static on the line. Sorry about that. Anna, I still love you. I want you back. Even after what you just told me, I still want you back. I feel so alone without you."

Anna listens to Nick and starts to cry. "Nick, why did you dump me? If you feel this way, why did you to that?" Anna thought. She returns her attention to the call as Nick says, "I hate going to sleep and waking up by myself. Everything I've done to try to get you out of my mind has failed. My focus, my concentration, my thoughts all involve you. I can't stop thinking about you. This doesn't feel right doing this over the phone. Can I see you? Even if it's just for a few minutes, I'd be happy with that."

Anna listens to Nick's pleas and can hear the sincerity in his voice. An image of Lisa enters Anna's mind and she smiles. Lisa is standing nude in front of Anna as she kisses Anna's neck and then she slowly transforms into Nick. Nick continues to kiss Anna's neck as he slides his hand down the side of her body, cupping her buttocks. They kiss passionately and hold each other.

Anna smiles as she fantasizes about Nick. She regains her focus and realizes that there is a car in front of her. She slams her foot on to the brake and her car makes a screeching sound. Anna looks in fear as her car slowly stops a couple of inches behind the car in front of her. Anna's heart races from her near-accident and she tries to calm herself. "Anna, are you still there?" Nick asks as Anna tries to slow down her heart rate form the near accident she had.

Anna looks at the street signs as she waits for the light to change. "Main Street and 14th Avenue. This is not too far from Nick's place. Maybe I should meet him in person and hear what he has to say" she thought. Nick checks his phone to see if the call has ended and thought, "The call hasn't ended. Why hasn't she answered? Can she hear me? Fucking piece of shit phone! AT&T sucks!" Anna adjusts herself in her seat and pulls over to a parking meter so she can talk to Nick.

Anna parks her car and exhales. "I can't believe I almost hit that car! I have to stop daydreaming" Anna thought. She looks at her dashboard and says, "Nick, I'm still on the phone. I was thinking about what you said and almost had an accident. I almost hit the car that was in front of me, but I stopped in time." Nick is worried and says, "Holy shit! Anna, are you OK? I'm sorry if I distracted you. Are you alright?"

The sound of concern from Nick's voice makes Anna smile. "He really does care about me" she whispers to herself. Anna puts the car in Park and asks, "Nick, are you home now?" Nick jumps out of his chair in excitement and says, "Yes, I'm home. Do you want to meet?" Anna smiles and says, "Yes. I'm only 5 minutes away from your place. Can I go there?" "Of course! I'll be here" Nick says in excitement. Anna says, "OK, see you soon" and presses the End Call button on her steering wheel to end the call.

Anna leans back in her seat and exhales. "I'll hear Nick out and see what he has to say. That's the least I can do. He saved my life. Nick cared for me when I was in the hospital. He's a passionate lover and really does care about me. Yes, he did dump me, but it had to be for a good reason, so I'll hear what he has to say" she thought. Anna puts the car into Drive and pulls out of the parking spot to drive to Nick's apartment.

Nick places his phone down on the table next to his chair and smiles. "Yes! She's coming over! Finally, after all this time! After all of the calls, emails and texts, she's finally going to hear me out. Her stupid fucking friends won't be around to influence her! We can finally have a real conversation. I can't stand her friends, especially Jane. She's such a fucking bitch!" Nick says. He looks at his phone and scrolls through his Photos until Anna's photo appears. Nick smiles and says, "You'll be mine again!"

Nick goes to the bathroom and examines his face. "That pimple finally cleared up" he thought as he leans towards the mirror to get a closer look at his face. He turns his head and nods in approval. "Good, that scar by my eye is almost gone. The surgeon really did a good job fixing that. I have to make sure my face doesn't get messed up if I want an acting career. The people at the movie studio said if I win the belt, I can use that to start a movie career. Those people make a lot of money without getting punched in the face" Nick thought and chuckles.

Nick looks at his reflection in the mirror and stares at himself. He says, "Don't fuck this up. You may only get this one chance to get her back." Nick reaches for his toothbrush, applies toothpaste on it and brushes his teeth. When he finishes brushing his teeth, Nick looks up at the mirror and says, "You still love Anna, even after everything that's happened while we were apart. I love her so much, I'm willing to forget about what she just told me."

Nick continues to brush his teeth as he thinks about Anna. He thought, "What if she's not coming back to you to get back together? Anna just left another man's bed! I'm getting excited for someone's sloppy seconds! No, don't think like that.

Remember, YOU left HER. She didn't cheat on you. We weren't together when she fucked another guy. Hey, I fucked around too after I broke up with Anna." Nick removes the toothbrush from his mouth, spits and rinses.

Nick places the toothbrush back into his mouth and brushes his teeth. He looks at the mirror and thought, "It's only fair that Anna slept with someone else after the break-up. I can't expect her to be a nun, she's too hot for that. Shit, I fucked this one girl that was crazy wild, but too clingy and emotional. Man she was hot! Nice legs, tits, ass, blonde-haired chick. What was her name? Damn, what was her name? Lisa! Yes, Lisa! That was her name! Damn! I have so much going on with this fight and the drama with Anna, I can't even remember a name! I need to start meditating some more so I can focus."

Nick spits out the toothpaste from his mouth and rinses. He fondly remembers the when he met Lisa. "The boys and I went to a bar and I were playing pool. Charlie just beat me and I went to the bar to get his drink since I lost the game. The bar was packed that night and I bumped into this hot little mama when I was leaving the bar. She almost fell and I felt so bad that I bought her a drink. Lisa was so fucking hot! If she were taller, she could be a model. If she wasn't so loca, who knows what could have happened with us?" he thought.

Nick reaches for a towel and wipes his mouth. He reaches for cologne and sprays his neck thinking, "Just a little, I don't want to smell like I bathe with this shit." After he sprays himself, Nick places the bottle back on the shelf on the side of the sink. He looks at the mirror again and smiles. Nick says, "I hope this works out. If it doesn't, I'm going to move on." He leaves the bathroom and returns to the living room.

Nick returns to the living room and sits. As Nick sits down, an image of Lisa enters his mind and he smiles. Lisa is in the shower and she invites him to join her. Nick enters the shower and Lisa transforms into Anna. "Who were you expecting?

Were you expecting someone else?" Anna asks and Nick shakes his head to stop his daydream. He sits in the chair, eagerly waiting for Anna's arrival.

Anna turns into the driveway of Nick's building. She turns down the radio and thought, "I wish I could park with the radio on! It's so hard to concentrate with the music blasting, it's distracting." Anna aligns her car into the parking space after turning the wheel several times. "The next car I get will have a rear-view camera. I'm sick of having to turn my body at different angles to back up my car" she thought. Anna stops the car, puts the shift lever into the Park position and reaches for her seatbelt buckle. As she reaches for the buckle, the speakers from the dashboard ring from an incoming phone call.

Anna looks at the dashboard screen and sees Lisa's name and phone number displayed. "Should I answer her call? She just kicked me out of her place. She was really angry at me because I took Nick's call. Maybe I should just let it go to voicemail. She scared me when she yelled at me earlier" Anna thought. The ringing sound from the dashboard stops and the sound of a chime is heard from the speakers.

Anna looks at the dashboard display and frowns. "She left me a voicemail. I'll listen to it later" Anna says and turns the key in the ignition to turn off the car. Anna exits her car and walks into the entrance of Nick's building. She enters the hallway leading to the elevators and thought, "This looks like the hallway in Lisa's building. I still don't know if I should tell Nick about her. Who know what will happen? He thinks that I slept with a man, not a woman."

Nick eagerly waits for Anna and rubs his hands together. He leans forward and looks at his phone, hoping that Anna doesn't call to cancel. "I really want to see Anna. I missed her so much! Even when I was with Lisa, I still thought about Anna. I couldn't stop thinking about her. If we get back together, Luis is just going to have to deal with it. He's going to have to accept that I love Anna and she's a part of my life" he thought. Nick leans back in his chair and an image of Lisa enters his mind.

Nick tries to dismiss this random thought, but he can't. Lisa is sitting at the edge of his bed, completely nude. Nick is looking down at Lisa's body, admiring it while cupping her breasts and rubbing her nipples. He can feel the warmth from Lisa's mouth as she inserts his penis into her mouth. Nick resists the urge to ejaculate as Lisa makes slurping sounds from moving her head back and forth on his penis.

Nick smiles as he remembers the last time he saw Lisa. He remembers how he stroked Lisa's long, silky hair as she sucked on his penis and grabbed his buttocks. Lisa would continue to suck on his penis until he ejaculated. Nick stops thinking about that night when he hears a knock at his door. He chuckles and says, "Damn that girl can give head! Well, that was then and this is now. Don't fuck this up." Nick gets up from the chair, adjusts his shirt and opens the door.

Anna stands in front of the door to Nick's apartment and pauses. "Should I tell him about Lisa or not? She made me do things, feel ways I never felt before with another woman. There's just something about her that attracts me to her. Enough about that, I'm here now in front of Nick's apartment. It's not too late to turn around, call Nick, cancel and go back to Lisa's place."

Anna walks away from Nick's door. She walks down the hallway and pauses. "Why am I thinking like this? I have to hear what Nick has to say. As much as I tried to forget about Nick, I can't. I can't stop thinking about him" Anna thought. She walks back to Nick's apartment and says, "OK, here we go" and exhales. Anna knocks on Nick's door and nervously waits for his arrival.

Nick opens the door and smiles at Anna. Anna smiles back at Nick, blushing with her legs crossed like a little school girl. Nick steps back from the door and stares at Anna. Anna nervously looks at Nick and asks, "Why are you staring at me?" Nick nervously says, "I was just admiring you. It feels like I haven't seen you for years. Your beauty captivates me." Anna blushes some more and jokingly says, "Always the romantic. Are you going to let me in or we're going to talk like this?" Nick chuckles and says, "Oh, of course! Please come in" and moves to the side so Anna can enter the apartment.

Anna enters Nick's apartment and immediately sits on the living room couch. Nick sits across from Anna and nervously smiles. They stare at each other briefly and Nick exhales. Nick and Anna lean towards each other and begin to speak at the same time. They say, "Anna, I..." "Nick, I..." and burst into laughter. Nick says, "OK, who goes first?" Anna says, "You can go first if you want to." Nick nods his head in agreement and says, "OK, I'll go first. I have a few things to get off of my chest." Anna leans back on the couch in anticipation of what Nick has to say.

Nick sits up in his chair, adjusting his posture so his back is straight and exhales. "Anna, I was wrong for what I did. What I did to you was cold, cruel and selfish. I made one of the biggest mistakes in my life." Anna sees the pain in Nick's face and reaches across the table to hold Nick's hand. "He really does feel bad about what he did. I had to see his face, his eyes to see if Nick is sincere. I keep forgetting that he's younger than me and can be impulsive" Anna thought. Nick fights back a tear and turns his hand so he can also hold Anna's hand.

Nick looks at Anna and is in awe. "From this angle, Anna looks like an angel. The way the light shines on her, I've never seen her like this. It's like she has a 'glow' coming from her. Seeing Anna here just makes me want her back that much more" Nick thought. Anna sees that Nick is hesitant to speak and whispers, "It's OK sweetie, I'm here. Tell me everything." Nick whispers, "God you're beautiful" and clears his throat.

Nick adjusts himself in his chair. He looks at Anna and says, "What I'm about to tell you, only a few people know. I want you to know that. You mean so much to me, I'm willing to tell you this." Anna looks at Nick and sees the seriousness in his eyes. She says, "OK, tell me everything." Nick looks at Anna and says, "Sam and Luis are like family to me. I knew Sam since we were kids. We grew up together in the same neighborhood. We did a lot of bad shit together. We used to rob drug addicts when they went to the park to buy crack or weed. We used to steal from the bodegas. We'd steal food, pampers, whatever wasn't nailed down just to survive."

Nick pauses for a moment and clears his throat. He leans back and says, "There was this one time Sam and I robbed this drug dealer that changed our lives. We went to the park really early in the morning to rob this crack dealer that was there to make a deal. We waited for the deal to be completed and attacked. The dealer pulled a gun on us and Sam was able to grab his arm. Sam broke the guy's arm and he almost stabbed Sam with a knife he hid in his belt. I saw the knife and was able to grab him from behind and...and..."

Anna sees the pain in Nick's face as the tears roll down his cheeks. "I broke his neck! I didn't know my own strength!" Anna is shocked by Nick's confession. She looks at Nick as he sobs and holds his hand to console him. Nick wipes his eyes and continues. "One day, Sam comes up to me and says that we're going to stop living that life. Sam was like my older brother and I listened to him. I followed him to Luis' gym. That gym was small, dark and dirty, but to us it became our church, our sanctuary, our home. Luis became our father. He took us in. He trained us, not just how to fight, but how to be men. Luis saved us from jail and the streets. That's why I couldn't lose him. That's why I chose him over you."

Nick leans back in his chair and wipes his tears. He stops crying and composes himself. Nick leans forward and asks Anna, "Would you like something to drink? My mouth is getting dry." Anna says, "Yes, water please" and Nick gets up from the chair. He goes to the kitchen and opens the refrigerator. Anna looks at

Nick as he goes to the kitchen and thought, "Oh my God! I never knew about this! I always thought Sam was exaggerating when he told me about his childhood. They were criminals! This is too much!"

Nick sees the concern in Anna's expression and sighs. "I hope this doesn't change her impression of me. I'm being honest with her and I hope that shows her I trust her" Nick thought. He looks at Anna and says, "It's obvious that Sam and I have some differences, but we both loved each other like brothers and loved Luis like our father. When you entered Sam's life, everything changed. Sam and Luis used to argue about you all of the time. If Sam wasn't such a great fighter, I don't think he would have beaten Thompson for the title. Anyway, one thing leads to another and you and I hook up" Nick says.

Nick closes the refrigerator door and returns to the living room. He hands Anna a bottle of water, sits down and drinks his water. Anna drinks her water and asks, "Does Luis know what happened?" Nick puts his bottle down on the table and says, "Yes, he knows. Luis didn't tell the cops about us. He knew that Sam and I didn't mean for that to happen. He knew that if we went to jail, our lives would be over."

Tears begin to flow from Nick's eyes as he speaks. He wipes them away and continues. "Luis taught us how to channel our aggression and use it productively. He made me into the man I am today. If I didn't do that, I'd probably be in jail or dead. I'll never stop thanking Luis for that." Anna looks at Nick and says, "You don't have to worry about me. Your secret is safe with me." Nick kisses Anna on the lips and says, "Thank you."

Anna's body tenses from Nick's kiss. She lets Nick kiss her again and leans on the couch. Nick stops kissing Anna and says, "You and I start dating and the whole time we were dating, I felt guilty for betraying Sam. I used to have nightmares about Sam and how he felt about us. The night that I was in the hospital and Luis found out that we were dating was just too much to deal with. I acted like a child, a coward. Instead of confronting Luis and professing my love for you, I let him bully me into leaving you. It was like losing my father all over again Anna. I couldn't bear to have that happen to me again, especially after what Luis did for me. I chose the easy way out. I ended our relationship so I can keep Luis in my life."

Anna looks at Nick as he buries his head in his hands and begins to sob. "I didn't know that Luis had that much of an impact on your life. I guess I would have done the same thing if my mother made me choose between you and her. So, what made you change? What happened that made you decide you want me back? Why do you want me back in your life now?" Anna asks. She looks at Nick as he rubs his hands, waiting for his answer.

Nick lifts his head up and wipes his tears. He reaches for the bottle of water and says, "It's simple. I love you. For the first time in my life, I have someone that I really care about. Someone that no matter what I'm doing, where I'm going, I'm always thinking about you. I tried to stop thinking about you, but couldn't. I'd be in the dojo training and your face would always be in my head. I would go to the supermarket, the Laundromat, the café and would see you there. I even went on a few dates with some other girl and couldn't stop thinking about you. Even when I was with her, I thought about you. Anna, I want you. I want you back in my life."

Anna smiles and holds Nick's hand. She asks, "What about Luis? What if he threatens to leave you again?" Nick shouts, "Fuck Luis! If he can't understand how happy you make me, then he can go fuck himself! He should be happy for me! Happy for us!" Nick leans towards Anna and kisses her on the lips. Anna returns Nick's kiss and they both stand up, moving closer to each other. They embrace and kiss passionately.

Anna and Nick kiss for several minutes. As Nick kisses Anna, he thought, "I hope this isn't what I think this is" as he tastes a salty residue from Anna's lips. He tries to avoid thinking about it, but the salty taste on Anna's lips makes him nervous. "Please tell me this isn't someone's cum that I'm tasting!" Nick thought. Anna kisses Nick and thought, "I hope he doesn't taste Lisa's cum from my mouth. She didn't give me a chance to freshen up."

Anna and Nick continue to kiss as they embrace. Anna looks at Nick and says, "Do you really want me back?" Nick smiles, picks up Anna in his arms and says, "Yes, with all of my heart" and kisses Anna again. Nick carries Anna towards his bedroom and Anna's phone rings.

Anna looks at Nick with a look of concern. Her phone continues to ring and he asks, "Anna, are you expecting a call?" Anna says, "No, let it go to voicemail" and Nick says, "OK." Nick places Anna on his unmade bed and Anna jokingly says, "You need to fire your maid, the bed hasn't been made." Nick says, "It won't need to be made after we're done" and smiles. Anna slides off her shoes, takes off her blouse and skirt, leaving only her bra and panties for Nick to remove. Nick crawls on top of Anna and jokingly says, "Let me see if I remember how to do this" using his teeth to remove Anna's pink lace thong.

Anna giggles and stops when her phone rings again. She frowns as Nick stops removing her thong and asks, "Do you want to see who is calling? Maybe it's important." Anna tries to hide her concerned look and looks at Nick. "This can't happen now! Everything's going back to normal and we're being interrupted by the phone! I hope that's not Lisa calling again. I'm here with Nick. She was a mistake. Being with her was a mistake. Yes, she made me cum and I'm attracted to her, but I want Nick!" she thought.

Anna turns her head back and forth and Nick says, "OK." He leans towards Anna's pelvis and grabs her lace thong with his teeth. Anna smiles and arches her body so Nick can slowly slide her thong off of her body. Anna reaches behind her back and unhooks her bra to remove it. She playfully tosses it on top of

Nick's head and he laughs. Nick places Anna's bra on his head, wearing it like a hat. He says, "How do you like my new head gear?" and Anna chuckles.

Anna's phone rings again and Nick is frustrated by the repeated calls. "It's like someone knows what we're doing and wants to stop us! It better not be the guy that she was just with. Let me find out who it is and I'm going to kick his ass!" he thought. Anna is annoyed by the sound of her phone and asks, "Can we stop for a moment so I can silence my phone?" "Thought you'd never ask" Nick says and moves off of Anna's body.

Anna sits up and slides off of the bed. She walks over to the living room as Nick stares at her buttocks, noticing several bruises on her cheeks. "What the fuck are those? Did she fall on her ass and bruise herself? I hope those aren't hickies! She did tell me that she just left someone else's place. Dammit! She probably this mother fucker's dick in her mouth and then comes over here and kisses me!" The thought of another man's penis in Anna's mouth makes Nick gag. Nick jumps out of the bed and runs into the bathroom to rinse his mouth.

Anna reaches for her purse and her phone stops ringing. She takes her phone out of her purse and sees three missed calls and voicemails from Lisa. "What the fuck? What is her problem? She kicks me out of her place then calls me non-stop! I wonder if she did this shit to Paul. I'm not going to return her calls, especially now" she thought. Anna presses the Volume button on her phone until the word "Vibrate" is displayed on the screen. "Good, now Nick and I won't hear the phone and stop being interrupted. I want to start over with Nick. A new start for both of us and no one is going to stop that" Anna thought.

Anna notices that Nick is not waiting for her on the bed and thought, "He's probably brushing his teeth." Anna walks over to the bathroom and hears Nick vomiting. "Honey, are you OK?" she asks. Nick forces himself to vomit into the toilet bowl and flushes. He stands up from the bowl, cups his hands under the stream of water so he can put the water into his mouth and spit it out. Nick repeats this several times then shuts off the water.

Anna is confused by Nick's actions and looks at Nick. She asks, "Honey, are you OK?" and Nick angrily says, "No, I'm not! How can you come over here after being with another man and not even freshen up? I think I tasted his cum on your mouth! I saw hickies on your ass when you went to your phone! I bet that was him calling you wasn't it? Don't just stare at me, answer me!"

Anna is angered by Nick's questions and grinds her teeth. She says, "First of all, *YOU* kissed *ME* knowing that I just came from someone else's place! Second, I had no idea I had hickies on my ass and third, it wasn't a *He* it was a *She* who I was with! Yes Nick, I fucked a woman! You drove me into the arms and bed of another woman, but I came back to *YOU*! Yes, that was her calling and I ignored her calls. Yes, she seduced me and made me cum, but I came back to *YOU*! Don't you understand you stupid little boy, **I WANT YOU!**"

Nick is angered and shocked by Anna's comments. He snaps his toothbrush in half from squeezing it and punches the mirror above the sink. Pieces of glass fall into the sink, showing Nick's reflection in each piece. He whispers, "You fucking bitch!" and Anna is scared. She reaches for her clothes and Nick storms out of the bathroom, grabbing Anna's hand. Anna lets go of her thong, letting it fall to the floor and looks at Nick in fear.

Anna's body trembles in fear as Nick looks her. Nick looks at Anna and says, "I'm sorry if I scared you. I was angry and had to let it out." Nick lets go of Anna's hand and she sits nervously on the bed. Nick sits on the opposite side of the bed and chuckles. He looks at Anna then looks away from her. "A woman. A woman. Jesus Christ. This is like a fucked-up soap opera" he says to himself. Anna turns to Nick and says, "I wanted to be honest with you. If we are going to be together again, I don't want any secrets between us."

Nick turns to look at Anna and chuckles. He holds Anna's hand and says, "IF we get back together. So I guess you have your doubts now. I'll admit, after our breakup, I messed around and started dating this one girl, but she was a psycho. At first, that turned me on, but then it got scary so I broke up with her. Damn blondes." When Nick says "blonds" an image of Lisa enters her mind. "Don't tell me Lisa was with Nick too! No, that can't be! That's too much of a coincidence" she thought.

Anna turns to speak to Nick when his phone rings. She sees the name displayed on the screen and mouths the words, "Oh shit!" Lisa's name and phone number displayed on the screen. Nick turns to look at his phone and sees that Lisa is calling him. "See what I'm talking about? That's her now. I asked her to stop calling me but she still calls" Nick says. He presses the Ignore button on the screen and focuses his attention towards Anna. She avoids looking at Nick, trying to hide her shocked expression. "I don't believe this! Not only did Lisa fuck Paul, she fucked Nick too! What the fuck?" she thought.

Anna is frozen in shock. "I can't believe this is happening. This is too much!" she thought. Nick looks at Anna and asks, "Are you OK? Look, I didn't know she was going to call. I told her to stop..." Anna interrupts Nick and says, "I think this was a bad idea. Look Nick, I don't think this is going to work between us." Nick angrily asks, "Is it because of her? You're a lesbian now? I don't make you happy anymore? What the fuck Anna?"

Anna starts to put on her clothes. She looks at Nick and says, "It's not you, it's me. I have a lot going on in my head and I need some space." Nick sighs and thought, "Jesus Christ! I just can't win here! I've had enough of this shit. Anna can go eat all of the pussy she wants, I'm done!" Nick sadly says, "Do what you want. You always do anyway" and walks out of the bedroom. Tears begin to flow from Anna's eyes as she quickly puts on her clothes.

Anna grabs her shoes and holds then in her hand as she leaves Nick's apartment. She stops to look at Nick as he sits on the couch and says, "I'm sorry." Nick doesn't reply and Anna leaves the apartment. Nick gets up from the couch and goes back into the bedroom. A chime sound is made from his phone and he sees that Lisa left a message on the phone. Nick looks at his phone and smiles. "If Anna won't be with me, I guess I have to do me" he says. Nick picks up the phone and says, "I wonder what Lisa said" as he presses the Play button to listen to the message.

VIII Confusion

Anna enters her car and leans back into the seat. Tears are pouring from her eyes, smearing her mascara, leaving black streaks down her face. She hits the steering wheel with the palm of her hand and sighs. "What was I thinking? I should have just went home and cleared my head, not go to Nick's place. How did this happen? Now I have no one. I never should have met Lisa. I never should have told Nick about Lisa. I don't need this shit!" Anna thought.

Tears continue to roll down Anna's face as she inserts the key into the ignition and starts her car. The dashboard lights up and displays the voicemail symbol. Anna sees there are several voicemails on her phone and pauses. "What does this bitch have to say? I've had enough of this fucking drama! This bitch has cost me so much in my life! I'm sick of her!" Anna shouts. She looks at the dashboard and says, "Play Voicemail." The dashboard says, "Playing first message" and Anna adjusts herself in her seat.

The sounds of crying and sniffling are heard throughout the car's speakers. Anna winces from the painful sounds of Lisa's crying and listens for several seconds until the message ends. Anna says, "Psycho bitch!" as she pulls out of the parking lot. As Anna begins to drive, the dashboard says, "Playing second message." The sound of Lisa's crying continues through the speakers and Lisa clears her throat. "Anna...Anna...please call me back. I over-reacted. I shouldn't have kicked you out. When I saw who was calling you I..." Lisa says as the message ends.

Anna sarcastically rolls her eyes as she listens to Lisa's messages. "What is wrong with her? Now I see what Nick was talking about. The girl is nuts!" Anna says. The dashboard says, "Playing third message" and Lisa's voice is now clearly heard on the speakers. Lisa says, "I saw Nick's name on your screen. I don't know if it's the same Nick that I know, but he's a fighter. We went out a few times. When I saw his name on your phone, I became angry. I hope you understand. He just dumped me, telling me he wants to get back with his old girlfriend. Seeing that name on your phone reminded me of him, so I took my anger out on you. I'm sorry. Please call me back."

Anna is shocked by Lisa's message. She slows down her car, almost to a complete stop. Several cars honk their horns at Anna, but she ignores them. "Well, that just confirms that Lisa did sleep with Nick. Holy shit! She was with Nick too! What the hell?" Anna thought. Angry motorists pass her by and shout at her. "Stop daydreaming bitch!" one driver shouts as he passes her car. Another driver passes her by and points his middle finger at Anna. She lowers her window and leans out of it. Anna shouts, "Fuck you!" to the driver and leans back in her seat.

Anna places her foot on the accelerator and speeds off. She passes through Stop signs and red lights. Anna arrives at her house and races into her driveway, leaving tire tracks on the pavement. "This is the one place I feel secure. I have to get away from all of this drama. This is too much to handle!" Anna thought. She puts the car in Park, turns the key in the ignition to turn off the car.

Anna exits the car, yawns and notices the tire tracks in her driveway. "Damn! How do I get rid of these? Great! Something else to deal with! I'll deal with that later" she thought. Anna's neighbor sees Anna staring at the tire tracks and jokingly asks, "Who are you running away from this time?" Anna smiles and says, "Everyone Bob, everyone." He says, "I hear you. You take care Anna" and goes back into his house.

Anna chuckles from her comment. She thought, "Everyone. Yes, that would be the best answer. I'm running from Nick, Lisa and myself." She opens the front door to the house and walks in. Anna sits on the couch and leans back on the cushions until she is comfortable. "I need to clear my head. Maybe some TV will help" she says. Anna turns on the large flat-panel television and presses the Up button on the remote to change the channel. Anna stops pressing the Up button when she sees a commercial for Nick's upcoming fight.

The television glows as bright lights and lettering fill the screen. A loud, booming voice is heard through the speakers as the commercial starts. "Ladies and Gentlemen, live from the casino in Las Vegas, Nevada, a fight extravaganza for the ages. The number one contender, the "comeback kid," Nick "Hard Head" Rodriguez gets his shot against the Heavyweight Champion of the World, John "Stone Hands" Walden. Watch it live on Pay Per View!" An image of Nick slamming Samuel to the ground is shown against an image of Walden punching a fighter in the face, making the fighter collapse. Anna winces from that image and thought, "I hope Nick is ready for that guy" and turns off the television.

Anna sighs out of frustration and tosses the remote to the side. "I need to take a long shower. I need to freshen up anyway" she says. Anna walks up the stairs to her bedroom while she takes off her clothes. She is at the top of the stairs when she hears her phone ring. Anna continues to take off her clothes and says, "Enough of this phone shit! I'll deal with it later! I've had enough drama today and I don't need any more! I need some time for myself and need to clear my head!"

Anna's phone rings several times then stops. She shouts, "Finally!" and turns on the water from the shower. Anna finishes undressing and stands completely nude in the bathroom. She looks at herself in the mirror and examines her face. Anna sees a sad reflection of herself. She looks away from the mirror and says, "I need to refresh myself. A nice, hot shower and some sleep will help me clear my head."

Anna steps into the shower and stands under the stream of water from the shower head. The water cascades down her body and Anna leans her head so the water can wet her hair. She reaches for the bar of soap that is resting on the side of the shower wall. Anna looks at the bar of soap and thought, "I'm going back to liquid soap. I don't like using the bar any more. It slips out of my hands and gets slimy when it sits in the soap dish. I don't care how much it's supposed to exfoliate my skin."

Anna holds the soap under the stream of water. A layer of foam appears on the soap and Anna begins to rub her body it. As Anna rubs her body, an image of Lisa enters her mind. Lisa is standing in the shower with Anna and says, "Let me help you with that." She takes the bar of soap from Anna and slowly moves it across Anna's body. Anna stands still as Lisa moves behind her. She closes her eyes as Lisa touches her skin. Lisa starts at Anna's shoulders, slowly rubbing them and the upper part of Anna's arms. Lisa rubs the soap against Anna's skin until a soapy layer of foam covers Anna's skin. Lisa nibbles on Anna's earlobe, creating a rush of excitement through Anna's body.

Lisa continues to move the bar of soap down Anna's body. She moves the soap towards Anna's breasts, much to her delight. Anna starts to breathe heavily as Lisa slowly moves her hand down her thigh. Anna's legs become tense from the sensation of Lisa's hand rubbing against them. Lisa whispers into Anna's ear, "Do you like this baby? Do you want me to continue?" Anna says, "Yes! Yes! Don't stop! Please don't stop!" Lisa kisses Anna's neck as she rubs the bar of soap slowly across Anna's left breast then her right breast. Anna moans in ecstasy as Lisa continues to move the bar of soap further down her body.

Lisa continues to move the soap and her hand down Anna's body. She moves her hand towards Anna's buttocks while using her other hand to rub the bar of soap down Anna's stomach. "I love how firm your body is. Your skin is so soft yet your body is so firm. It just turns me on" Lisa says. She massages Anna's buttocks and kisses Anna on the lips.

Anna drops the bar of soap from her hands. She begins to rub her breasts with her left hand and rubs her clitoris with her right hand. Anna moves her body so the stream of water from the shower head hits her stomach, then her vagina. She rubs her nipples on her breasts until they are erect and Anna hums. "Oh fuck this feels good!" she thought. Anna inserts her fingers inside of her vagina and moans.

Lisa's image returns and Anna smiles. Lisa's hand is now at Anna's vagina, rubbing her clitoris. Anna spreads her legs so Lisa can reach her vagina. "This feels so good!" Anna shouts. Lisa smiles and whispers, "You like this mamí? Tell me you want me. Tell me you want more. I know you want me as much as I want you." Anna opens her mouth to answer when the shower curtain opens. Anna and Lisa pause as Nick opens the shower curtain and asks, "Can I join you ladies? You can't have all of the fun here." Anna and Lisa smile and say, "Come on in."

Anna continues to stand under the stream of water, fantasizing about Lisa and Nick. Nick enters the shower, closing the curtain behind him. Nick moves behind Anna while Lisa moves in front of Anna, rubbing her clitoris. Anna massages Lisa's breasts while Nick places his hand by Anna's clitoris. Nick and Lisa begin to rub Anna's clitoris at the same time while Nick kisses Anna's neck. Anna removes one of her hands from Lisa's breast and reaches back so she can massage Nick's penis. Nick turns Anna's head so he can kiss her passionately. Lisa kisses Anna's neck and slowly moves down Anna's neck, reaching Anna's breasts.

Anna smiles and bites her lip as she continues her fantasy. She slowly moves her hand towards her vagina and rubs her clitoris. The fantasy returns as Lisa licks Anna's firm, erect nipples while Nick inserts his index finger into Anna's vagina. Anna looks at Nick and shouts, "Fuck me! Fuck me hard!" Nick and Lisa remove their hands from Anna's vagina so she can bend over. Nick slowly inserts his penis into Anna's vagina while Lisa squats in front of Anna. Lisa tilts her head and licks Anna's vagina with her tongue, also holding Nick's penis as it slides in and out of Anna's vagina.

Anna continues to insert her fingers into her vagina as her fantasy continues. She quickens her pace until she screams in pleasure, releasing her warm ejaculation on to her hand. Anna leans back against the shower wall, gasping for air from the intensity of her orgasm. "Holy shit! I have never came like that in my life! Oh my God that was so fucking good! Whew!" Anna shouts. She rinses off the remaining soap from her body and turns off the shower just as the water turns cold. She stands in the shower for a couple of minutes to regain her breath.

Anna exhales and reaches for a towel. She steps out from the shower and begins to dry herself. "That was intense! I can't believe that I imagined that! Lisa and Nick at the same time! My hand really wanders sometimes. I can't believe I'm in the same situation again! Do I go back to Nick or go back to Lisa? I barely know Lisa, but I've never felt such a connection to someone since I met Paul. I still care about Nick. He's sweet, gentle and even though he's younger than Sam, he's much more mature. This is too much!" Anna thought.

Anna dries herself and wraps the towel around her body. She sits on her bed and thought, "Could I have both of them? What if I can make my fantasy a reality? Would they agree to that? No! That's really reaching Anna! Oh Jesus Christ! What do I do here?" Anna lies back on the bed and stares at the ceiling. She tosses and turns on the bed and says, "I need to talk to someone about this." Anna thinks for a moment and says, "Jane! She's always been there for me and she's open-minded. I'll call her."

Anna reaches into her purse that she threw on her bed earlier and grabs her phone. Anna presses the Contacts button on the screen and presses on Jane's name. She eagerly waits for Jane to answer as the phone rings. Anna says, "Come on Jane, please answer. I really need you now." Jane answers the call and says, "Hi Anna! How's my girl? What have you been up to?" The sound of Jane's voice makes Anna smile.

Anna sits up in her bed and clears her throat before answering Jane. She exhales and says, "Jane, I'm good. Actually, I'm not 100% good." "What's wrong? Are you OK? What happened?" Jane asks. Anna replies, "I need to talk to you about something. This is very awkward, but I really need some advice about this. Remember that I was supposed to meet Lisa, the girl that Paul had an affair with?" "Yes, that little bitch you saw at the club. I hope you beat the shit out of her. If you're in jail, just tell me where you are and how much is the bail, I'll get you out of there."

Anna smiles from Jane's comment. "Jane is always there for me, no questions asked. How many people would offer to bail me out of jail without hesitation? Jane's the best" she thought. Anna chuckles and says, "No, I'm not in jail. I met Lisa and something happened. Well, let me back up and give you the complete story. When I saw Lisa at the club, I went to confront her and she...she...hit on me. Lisa thought I was a lesbian and I followed her into the bathroom to 'hook up.'"

Jane is stunned by what Anna just told her. "What the fuck? I hope this is a bad joke! This is so fucking weird!" she thought. Jane says, "What? Holy shit! That little slut! Jesus Christ, she'll fuck anything! No offense." Anna says, "None taken. Well, here's the odd part, Lisa kissed me in the bathroom and I didn't stop her." Jane is in shock and at a loss for words. A period of silence passes and Anna asks, "Jane are you still there?" Jane answers, "Yes, I'm here. Just...shocked. I'm having a hard time processing this. Jesus Christ! Ayúdame Díos...so, what happened next?"

Anna is nervous about revealing further details about Lisa to Jane. "Jane is my girl, but she can only be so supportive. Maybe I shouldn't tell her. No, don't do that. I trust Jane. She's always been there for me" Anna thought. Anna adjusts herself and says, "We spoke and decided to meet up to talk about everything that happened. I met her earlier today and I didn't know what came over me, but I wound up at her place and we had sex." Jane is in disbelief and shock. "Can you repeat that? You had sex with her? With Lisa? Jesus Christ!" Jane says.

Anna winces from Jane's reaction and continues. "When Lisa and I finished, Nick called my phone and I want to his place. I told him I slept with another woman and we argued. I left his place and while going back home, Lisa left me a message telling me that she dated Nick" Anna tearfully says. Jane moves the phone away from her ear so Anna can't hear her say, "What the fuck?" Jane places the phone back to her ear and says, "Wow! For once in my life, I don't know what to say! This is a lot to take in Anna. Wow!"

Anna eagerly waits for Jane's advice. "Jane's always been a voice of reason for me. She can help me with this situation. I hope she can help me" Anna thought. Jane pauses for a moment then says, "So let me get this right so everything's clear. You were dating Nick, break up, hook up with Paul's mistress then try to get back with Nick. So you don't know if you want to be a lesbian or get back with Nick, am I right?"

Anna winces when Jane says "lesbian." She says, "Yes, that's correct. Should I go back to Nick, go to Lisa or just say 'fuck it' and don't choose anyone and move on?" Anna waits for Jane's reply as she sits on the bed. Jane pauses and says, "Anna, give me a minute to think." Jane bites her lip in frustration. She thought, "If this was anyone else, I'd say that I can't help them and end the call. Her drama can really stress me out. Jesus Christ, Anna, what is wrong with you? Anna, you're too much sometimes!"

Jane places her phone down and sighs. "Anna, why do you put yourself in these situations? Why couldn't you just move on?" she thought. Jane picks up the phone and says, "Anna, Anna, Anna. You and your love drama. I thought that after the whole mess with Sam and Paul, you would have learned from that." Jane pauses to adjust herself in her chair and says, "Anna, before I answer you, I have to tell you something." Anna says, "Oh no, please don't tell me it's bad news!" "No, nothing like that. I've never told anyone about this, but when I was in high school, I slept with another girl in my class" Jane says.

Jane's revelation shocks Anna. "Holy shit! First Susan, now Jane! Who's next, Miriam? Is this something that most women do?" Anna thought. She says, "Holy shit! I don't believe it! Why didn't you tell me?" Jane pauses and says, "It was my dirty little secret. I was young and curious. It sounds cliché, but it's true."

Anna is at a loss for words. She listens to Jane as she speaks. Jane says, "We always liked each other, but one night we were smoking weed together and started experimenting. One thing led to another and we had sex. To be honest, all I can chalk to up to is experience because I didn't enjoy it. I prefer men. Now on to you, what you did with Lisa, was that curiosity or do you actually feel something towards her?" Jane asks.

Anna sighs and thinks about Jane's question. "Do I actually care about Lisa or was she just a fling? What about Nick? I still love him. Seeing him today just made me want him even more, but Lisa is so beautiful and dominant, she just turns me on" she thought. Anna says, "I honestly don't know. I like both of them. Obviously, I know Nick longer and still love him, but there's just something about Lisa that I can't stop thinking about her."

Jane waits for Anna to stop so she can respond. "Anna can be really selfish at times and needs to be clear about what she wants" she thought. Jane says, "Anna, you're just confused. You slept with Lisa and it's a new experience for you. You enjoyed being with Lisa so you want more. I think that once you start seeing Nick again, you'll forget about Lisa. Remember, she's the woman that Paul had an affair with. Nick genuinely cares about you.

Besides, it's not like you can have both of them. If you try that, someone will get hurt."

Anna sits up on her bed and yawns. She thinks about what Jane said, "Someone will get hurt" and returns her attention back to Jane. Anna says, "Jane, thanks for this. You know you're the only person I can really talk to. Thanks a lot." "No problem sweetie. You take care and hopefully whatever decision you make will make you happy." Anna says, "Thanks again. Take care." Anna presses the End Call button on her screen and places the phone next to her on the bed. Anna lies back on the bed and stretches so she is comfortable. "Lisa or Nick, Nick or Lisa or none of them. 'Whatever decision makes you happy' Jane says. Maybe I can have both of them. Nick AND Lisa. Lisa AND Nick" Anna thought as she closes her eyes and falls asleep.

IX Fight Night

"You're gonna tear into Walden and make him bleed! You're gonna beat this mother fucker and bring that belt back home! You're the next champ Nick!" Luis shouts as he wraps Nick's hands. Nick sits on the bench in his private dressing room and tries to focus on his fight. "I have to stop thinking about Anna and Lisa. They both fucked my head up that day" he thought.

Nick looks at Luis as his hands are being wrapped. Luis speaks to Nick and his words are silent as Nick thinks about Anna and Lisa. "Anna sleeps with another woman, comes to my place to get back together then leaves. Lisa calls me after Anna leaves and wants to hook back up. She tells me that she's sorry about everything. I don't need that drama in my life now. I almost lost my last fight because I was thinking about Anna. I have a chance to win the title tonight and nothing is going to stop me!" he thought.

Luis looks at Nick and smiles. He says, "I know we had some problems, but I'm glad that's behind us. Nick, I'm very proud of you. You have the heart of a warrior! You would make Sam proud! This is your time! You earned this! Go out there and bring our belt back home!" Nick smiles and nods his head in agreement. Luis leans forward and hugs Nick saying, "I love you kid, you're the best." Nick says, "Love you too Luis" and hugs him.

An image of Sam enters Nick's mind and he tears up. Luis looks at Nick and asks, "Thinking about Sam?" Nick tearfully says, "Yes. I wish he could be here to see this." Luis holds back a tear and says, "He is kid. He's looking down at us and wants you to win back his belt. Bring it back to the family where it belongs." Luis finishes wrapping Nick's hands and smiles. "You're the best kid. I believe in you. Sam believed in you. Now go out there and win!" he says. Nick smiles and pounds his fists together to ensure the wrappings are comfortable.

Nick and Luis stand up and prepare to enter the octagon. Luis helps Nick put on his robe and asks, "Ready champ?" Nick says, "Ready" and when Luis reaches for the door knob, Nick's phone rings. Luis says, "Ignore it, let's go" and Nick complies. Nick looks around the hallway and remembers when he was with Sam. Sam, Luis and Nick all walked down that hallway towards the octagon when Sam defended his title. "Sam was so intense. He took his anger out on Thompson that night." Nick stops thinking about that night and returns his focus to his fight.

Lisa stands in her living room pacing back and forth as she waits for Nick to answer her call. "Why won't he pick up? I want to wish him good luck for his fight. Damn! Voicemail! I'll leave a message" she thought. "Nick, it's Lisa. I was hoping I could talk to you before your fight. I just wanted to wish you good luck tonight with your fight. I hope you win tonight and if you feel up to it later, call me so we can meet. I have a special treat for you. I miss you. I want to see you" Lisa says.

Nick walks down the hallway with Luis towards the octagon. The cheers from the crowd resonate down the hallway. The chant, "Hard Head, Hard Head!" is heard down the hallway and they smile. Luis says, "See Nick! That's for you! The people want you to be the champ! Do this for them! Do this for me! Do this for Sam! Most of all, do this for yourself!" Nick smiles and says, "You got it coach!" and jogs in place so he can maintain his body temperature while waiting for the announcement of his entrance.

The ring announcer walks to the center of the octagon and the crowd cheers. "Ladies and Gentlemen, this is the main event of the evening! This contest is scheduled for five rounds and it is for the Heavyweight Championship of the World! Introducing first, the challenger..." A spotlight shines at the entrance and the song "Walk" from Pantera booms throughout the building.

Luis and Nick look at each other and smile. "Ready champ?" Luis asks. Nick says, "Born ready!" The crowd sings along with the song as Nick, Luis and the corner men walk towards the octagon. "Here is the challenger, from Brooklyn, New York, weighing 225 pounds with a record of 15 wins, 2 defeats, all wins by way of submission, the number one contender, Nick "Hard Head" Rodriguez!" The crowd cheers as Nick enters the octagon.

The lights in the building dim and the song "Search and Destroy" from Metallica resonates throughout the building. The crowd cheers as the champion starts to walk towards the octagon. "Ladies and Gentlemen. Presenting the reigning, undefeated Heavyweight Champion of the World, from San Francisco, California, weighing 235 pounds with a perfect record of 16 wins, no defeats, all by way of knockout, John "Stone Hands" Walden!" Walden enters the octagon and looks at Nick with an intense stare.

As Nick and Walden walk towards the center of the octagon, Anna sits at the edge of her couch. She watches the referee give instructions to the fighters and says, "I hope Nick wins. He almost lost his last fight." The color commentator says, "Look at the intensity in their eyes! You can tell that they both want to win. Rodriguez, the submission specialist who can also take a punch, hence the name 'Hard Head' and Walden the striker. This is a classic grappler versus striker match up. I can't wait for it to start!" The referee walks to the center of the octagon and starts the fight.

The crowd erupts as Nick and Walden approach each other. An image of Anna and Lisa enters Nick's mind and he quickly dismisses it. Walden throws a few jabs at Nick and Nick moves side to side, avoiding Walden's jabs. Walden throws a wild right hand at Nick. Nick lowers his body, avoiding Walden's punch and grabs his legs. Anna gets off of her couch in excitement and shouts, "Go Nick, go!" Nick lifts Walden off of the canvas and slams him down. He grabs Walden's arm and twists it. "Oh my God! Rodriguez just shot in on Walden as is going for a Key Lock!"" the commentator shouts.

The crowd erupts as Nick tries to make Walden submit to his hold. Anna jumps up and shouts, "Get him Nick! Get him!" Luis shouts at Nick, "Side control, side control!" and Nick moves his body so he is now lying across Walden's body, pinning him so he can't move. Walden frees his arm from Nick's hold and tries to turn his body so he can attempt to stand up. Nick sees that Walden's neck is exposed from turning his body and immediately attacks. Nick wraps his arms around Walden's neck, placing him in a choke hold.

Anna watches intently at Nick's fight, moving closer to the television and cheering. "You have him Nick! Don't let him go!" Anna shouts at the television. Nick squeezes Walden's neck and wraps his legs around Walden's waist so he can't escape the choke hold. The referee stands above them and watches. Walden taps on Nick's leg, signaling that he submits. The referee pulls Nick's arms apart and tells Nick, "Fight's over, you won." Nick removes his legs from Walden's body and stands up. Luis runs into the octagon and hugs Nick, celebrating Nick's victory. Anna jumps up and down in front of her television and cheers. "Yes! Yes! Yes! He did it! Nick's the champ!"

Luis hugs Nick as tears of joy flow from their eyes. Nick walks over to the center of the octagon and the referee raises his hand in victory, much to the delight of the crowd. The commissioner enters the octagon and places the championship belt around Nick's waist. The ring announcer says, "Ladies and Gentlemen, the winner by way of rear naked choke in two minutes and fifteen seconds in the first round, and NEW Heavyweight Champion of the World, Nick 'Hard Head' Rodriguez!"

Nick collapses to his knees and cries. Luis walks over to Nick and him again. "I told you kid, you're the champ! I'm proud of you! Let's do this interview and get out of here." The color commentator enters the octagon and walks over to Nick and Luis. "Champ! Let me be the first to publicly congratulate you on your impressive win tonight! During your time here, we've seen you grow into the champion that you are and I think I speak for everyone here and say we're all proud of you!"

Nick steps away from Luis and the commentator. He starts to cry and looks up at the ceiling whispering, "This was for you Sam!" He returns to the center of the octagon and says, "Thanks Joe. That means a lot to me. Winning this belt means so much to me. I did this for Luis, I did this for the fans and I did this in honor of the man who will always be the champion..." Nick starts to choke up and composes himself. He says, "I did this for my brother Sam!"

Nick stands in the middle of the octagon and looks at the crowd. He shouts, "I love you Sam! This one's for you!" The crowd cheers and chants "Sam! Sam! Sam!" and everyone standing in the octagon, including Walden tear up. Walden walks up to Nick and hugs him, raising his hand in victory. The crowd cheers as Walden bows to Nick and applauds. Nick smiles and returns the bow, showing mutual respect to Walden.

Nick takes off his championship belt. He places it on his shoulder, holding it proudly. Nick looks at Walden and says, "Thanks Champ. Thank you for this opportunity" and Walden says, "You're welcome Champ. I'll see you at the rematch" and exits the octagon. Nick says, "You got it Champ!" and Walden gives Nick a thumbs up.

Anna turns off the television and sits back down. "I'm so happy for Nick. He worked so hard. He deserves this. I should call him to congratulate him. We haven't spoken since that day I was at his place and I want him to know that I saw his fight" she thought. She looks at the phone and takes note of the time.

Anna thought, "He'll probably take about 30 to 45 minutes to take off his wrappings, shower and get dressed. Since he won tonight, he'll have a press conference. That will take about 30 minutes to finish so I'll call him in an hour."

Nick returns to his dressing room and immediately goes to his locker. He reaches for his phone and sees a missed call, a voicemail and a text message from Lisa. "So much for easing up on the calls" he thought. Nick presses the Voicemail button on his phone and listens to Lisa's message. After listening to the message, Nick smiles. He says, "Maybe I will see her." He removes the phone from his ear and looks at the text that Lisa sent.

Nick's smile widens as he looks at his phone. A picture of Lisa standing completely nude with the message, "Come and get it Champ! Claim your prize!" is displayed on his phone. Nick chuckles and Luis walks over to Nick. "Champ, you did really good out there. Let me unwrap your hands" Luis says. Luis carefully cuts the layers of tape that hold the wrapping around Nick's hands. Nick looks at Luis and says, "I couldn't have done this without you Luis. I love you." Luis smiles and says, "Love you too kid" and Nick's phone rings.

Anna picks up her phone and calls Nick. "He should be able to answer now" she thought. Ana eagerly waits for Nick to answer her call as she plays with her hair. "He should be getting ready to leave by now. I hope he takes my call" she thought. Nick looks at his phone and sees Anna's picture and name displayed on the screen. He smiles briefly then looks at Luis. "Anna probably watched the fight tonight. Let's see what she has to say" he thought.

Luis sees the screen out of the corner of his eye and is angered. He looks at Nick and says, "I thought you and Anna broke up." Nick says, "We did. I don't know why she's calling. She's probably calling to congratulate me. Besides, I got a call and a text from Lisa and I may go to her place later." Luis smiles and jokingly says, "OK Champ, just remember to ask Lisa if she has an older friend she can introduce me to." Nick laughs and says, "You're a dirty old man!" Luis jokingly says, "I'll be one until I'm a dead old man!" and they both laugh.

Nick presses the Answer button on his phone and can hear Anna breathing. Anna hears Nick breathing and is excited. "Nick, it's Anna. I saw the fight and wanted to congratulate you. I'm so happy for you and proud of you! You've worked so hard for this and it paid off. You were so dominant tonight. You really looked good out there" she says. Nick smiles and thought, "She's on my dick now that I'm the Champ, figures." Luis finishes removing the wraps from Nick's hands and says, "I'll give you some privacy" and walks away, patting Nick on the shoulder.

Nick looks at his newly won championship belt and smiles. "I'm the Champ. Now everyone wants to be with the Champ, including Anna and Lisa" he thought. Nick places the phone next to his ear and says, "Thanks Anna, I appreciate that." Anna is surprised at the coldness of Nick's tone. "He sounded like he didn't want to talk to me, like I meant nothing to him" she thought. A moment of silence passes and Nick says, "OK Anna, I have to go. I'm going to take a shower, have my press conference and get out of here. You take care." Anna starts to cry and tearfully says, "OK, you take care" and ends the call.

Nick looks at his phone and presses on the Messages button. He opens the attachment that Lisa sent him and smiles. He looks at the photo that Lisa sent him and says, "Everyone wants to be with the Champ." He places his phone back into the locker and removes his ring gear. Luis walks over to Nick and asks, "Is everything OK?" Nick says, "I'm good. I'm going to hit the shower, get out of here and celebrate." Luis nods his head and walks away.

Anna slowly places her phone down on the table in front of her and sobs. "He was so cold! I thought he'd be happy I called! Happy I watched his fight! Did he move on already? Did he find someone else? What if Lisa got back with him? No, I don't think she wants to go back to him. Maybe Nick is angry at me and needs some time alone. I don't know any more" she thought. Anna grabs her phone and goes up to her bedroom. Anna lies on her bed and looks at the photo of Nick that is on the nightstand. She says, "Love you" and rests her head on a pillow, falling asleep.

X Payback

Nick steps into the showers and turns on the water. He stands to the side of the water and extends his hand so he knows when the water is warm. As Nick waits for the water to warm up, he thought, "I can't wait to get out of here! Lisa looks so good in that picture! I'll call her and 'claim my prize' like she says." Nick moves under the stream of water and an image of Lisa enters his mind.

Lisa is slowly removing her clothes as she dances in front of him. Nick sits on his bed, smiling and laughing as Lisa tosses her bra at him. The image of Lisa disappears as Nick turns his body so the hot water hits different areas of his body to relax his muscles. The image of Lisa returns as Nick stretches under the water. Lisa removes her panties, rubbing them between her legs and tosses them at Nick, much to his delight.

Nick playfully pretends to throw money at Lisa as she gets on her hands and knees. She poses for Nick in different positions on the floor as Nick removes his shirt. Lisa crawls towards Nick, reaching for his belt buckle to remove it. Nick smiles as the water strikes his face and he begins to rub soap on his body. "I can't wait to see Lisa" he thought.

Lisa looks at her phone in anticipation of Nick's call. "I hope he saw my text. It's really hard to pose like that and take a selfie. When I saw him on the news tonight choking that guy, he really turned me on. Nick looked so good, I just have to see him. I miss him a lot, even though I'm pretty sure he called Anna that day. I know that Anna dated Nick before I did and it's her loss. She could have had Nick, she could have had me, but she blew it! She's such a selfish bitch!" she thought.

Lisa takes a sip from the glass of wine that is next to her and places it back on the table. She thought, "Anna thinks that she can be with anyone she wants and treat them like shit! Well Anna, you lose, I win! Nick will hear that message, look at my pictures and come to me! Nick and I were meant to be together!" She gets up from the chair and stretches. Lisa looks at the clock on the wall and says, "Damn Nick, call me already! Your fight ended an hour ago!"

Lisa walks over to her bedroom and uses her hand to smooth the sheets on the bed. She goes into her dresser drawer and pulls out a lighter and a scented candle. "Nick likes this. He told me that the smell makes him relax and feel at ease" she says and places the lighter and candle on the bedside table. Lisa's phone rings and she runs towards the living room. She almost trips on a shoe that is lying on the floor. "Fuck! I almost broke my neck!" she shouts.

Lisa looks at her phone and smiles when she sees Nick's name on the screen. Lisa presses the Answer button and says, "Hi sweetie! Congrats! How's my champion? Did you get my text?" Nick smiles and looks at his championship belt. "I'm the Champ!" he whispered to himself and returns his attention back to his phone. He presses the Speaker button on the phone and opens the picture that Lisa sent him.

Nick looks at his phone and stares at the photo Lisa sent to him. "Damn she's fine! I'm going to celebrate tonight!" he thought. Nick smiles and says, "Yes, I got it. I see you're still shaving." Lisa blushes and says, "You naughty boy! When are you coming over?" Nick jokingly says, "I didn't recall saying 'yes.' You can't assume that just because you sent me this very naughty photo that I'll come running. I need to be wined and dined too." Lisa says, "Shut up wise ass! Get over here already!" Nick smiles and says, "I'll be there soon" and ends the call.

Lisa places her phone down and licks her lips. She looks at the clock and yawns. "God it's late. I want to sleep, but Nick is coming over. If he thinks that old woman can fuck, want till he sees what I can do! If Anna thinks she knows how to fuck, let's see what a younger, sexier woman can do! I'll show her! I'll win Nick back and he'll never be hers again! That'll show that bitch!" she thought. Lisa walks into the bathroom and looks at herself in the mirror, admiring herself. "I look so good, I'd fuck me" she jokingly says.

Lisa takes of her t-shirt and panties. She puts on a robe and looks at the mirror again. "I want to be with Nick. I have to win him back. I hope he shows up soon, I'm tired" she thought. She returns to the living room and sits on the sofa, eagerly waiting for Nick. "I can't believe Anna and I both slept with the same man, twice! First Paul, now Nick! Well, this time, I'm keeping the man! What was I thinking when I seduced Anna? She looks great for her age, but she's too selfish" Lisa thought.

Lisa looks at her phone and yawns. "Sometime today Nick! I want to show Nick that I am better than Anna in every way. I will admit that for a woman her age, she does look fine and she made me cum really hard. Why am I thinking about her? Nick is coming over and I'm thinking about Anna's firm breasts and nice round ass. Her ass was so round, I nibbled on both of her cheeks. I think I left hickies on her ass. It was like biting into an apple" Lisa thought and smiled.

Lisa's phone rings and she sees Nick's name on the screen. She answers the phone and Nick says, "I'm almost there. I had to stop for some fans who waited for me. I signed a few autographs and took pictures with the fans. There must have been 100 people waiting for me there. That's what made me late. I can't let my fans down. I'll probably get there in the next 5 to 10 minutes." "OK baby, I'll be waiting" Lisa says with a smile.

Nick's car arrives at Lisa's building and he yawns. "Man I'm tired!" he says as the driver parks in front of the building. "Champ, do you want me to wait for you or should I come back later?" the driver asks. Nick says, "Wait here for a few minutes and I'll call you to let you know what's going on." The driver says, "OK Champ" and Nick exits the car. Nick walks into the building and presses the button labelled "106" for Lisa's apartment. Lisa runs over to the intercom and presses the button so Nick can enter. "He's finally here! I almost fell asleep waiting for him! I hope I still have energy for Nick. I'm going to make him mine!" she thought.

Nick walks down the hallway to Lisa's apartment and smiles when she opens the door. Lisa stands with her door and robe partially open. The right side of Lisa's body is exposed, showing off Lisa's leg and part of her breast. Nick sees Lisa's body and smiles. He reaches for his phone and calls the driver. "You can leave, I'll be here for a while" Nick says as Lisa blows a kiss at him. The driver says, "OK Champ. Enjoy the rest of your evening" and Nick smiles.

Lisa opens the door and jumps on top of Nick. She kisses Nick on the lips as she wraps her legs around his body. He enters Lisa's apartment and closes the door behind him. Nick thought, "Holy shit is Lisa aggressive! Is this because she misses me or because I'm the Champ? Nick, stop thinking for a moment and look at where you are. You're at Lisa's place and you're going to fuck her like there's no tomorrow. You deserve it."

Lisa continues to kiss Nick as he carries her into the bedroom. He sits on the bed with Lisa's legs still wrapped around his body. When Nick sits on the bed, Lisa unwraps her legs from his body so she can remove her robe. Lisa pushes Nick back so he is lying on the bed and she sits on top of him. Nick looks up at Lisa and asks, "Did you miss me?" Lisa playfully slaps Nick in the face and says, "Shut up bitch! You shut up and do as I say!"

Lisa grabs Nick's genitals, massaging the bulge in his jeans. Nick smiles and thought, "OK, I'll play along. Let her dominate me. I like this side of Lisa. She knows what she wants and how to get it. She really turns me on when she takes control.

Sometimes it's nice to let someone else take control. Besides, I'm really tired." Nick's penis slowly becomes erect, much to Lisa's delight. She continues to massage Nick and thought, "Now to really turn him on!"

Lisa unzips Nick's jeans and unbuckles his belt. She removes Nick's belt and playfully whips him with it. "Not too hard sweetie" Nick says and Lisa puts her left foot on his face. She shouts, "Shut up bitch! You keep your mouth shut!" and places her toes into Nick's mouth. Nick licks and sucks on Lisa's toes as she slides his pants off one leg at a time. Lisa moves her foot around Nick's face as he playfully tries to grab her foot. She smiles and giggles as Nick nibbles on her toes and thought, "He's mine Anna! I'll make sure you know Nick is mine!"

Lisa leans back and reaches for her phone. Lisa scrolls through her Contacts until Anna's name appears on the screen. Nick leans his head forward to see what Lisa is doing and she pushes his head back with her foot. Lisa shouts, "Did I say you can get up? Stay still bitch!" Nick chuckles and complies with Lisa's command. She presses Anna's name on the screen and thought, "Anna will never try to win Nick back after she hears this!"

Anna's phone rings and she turns her body towards the sound of the phone. She reaches for her phone and sees Lisa's name displayed on the screen. The bright light from the screen makes Anna squint her eyes. "I have to dim that Brightness setting on the phone! I can't believe this is hurting my eyes!" Anna thought. She looks at the phone and says, "Great! It's Lisa, whoopee! She's probably drunk-dialing me" and goes back to sleep.

Lisa looks at her phone as she continues to remove Nick's clothes. "She's not answering! Fuck! She's probably asleep. Well, she's going to have one hell of a voicemail" she thought. Lisa removes her foot from Nick's mouth and Nick tries to adjust his body. Lisa grabs Nick's chin and shouts, "You move when I tell you bitch!" and shoves his head back on the pillow. Nick grunts as Lisa forces his head back on the pillow. She says, "Oh, you didn't like that?" and starts to massage Nick's penis again.

Lisa continues to remove Nick's clothes. She lifts up Nick's shirt slowly as she licks his stomach, moving up to his chest. Nick lowers his head back on to the pillow and thought, "Now that's more like it! That's what I want!" Lisa shouts at Nick, "Take off your shirt and finger my pussy!" Nick complies with Lisa's command, removing his shirt and slowly moves his hand towards Lisa's vagina. He begins to rub Lisa's clitoris and Lisa moans. She shouts, "Oh yes Nick! Just like that! Rub my pussy and make it wet! Make this pussy yours!"

As Lisa moans and shouts, her phone stays connected to the call she placed to Anna. The seconds continue to increase on the call as Lisa continues. She adjusts her body so she is facing Nick's penis and Nick can now rub Lisa's vagina from behind. Nick inserts two of his fingers into Lisa's vagina and she moans. Lisa starts to lick on Nick's penis shouting, "Nick, your cock is so hard! I love sucking your cock! Do you want me to suck your cock? Answer bitch!" Nick smiles and says, "Yes! Yes! I want you to suck my cock!"

Lisa smiles as Nick answers her. "Good! He said that loud enough so it can be on the voicemail" she thought. Lisa inserts Nick's penis into her mouth and uses her tongue to lick the top of it. She spreads her legs so Nick can insert more of his fingers into her vagina and slides one of his fingers into her anus. Lisa moans and shouts, "Yes Nick! Just like that! Finger my pussy and my ass! Ahh!" Nick continues to slide his fingers in and out of Lisa's vagina and anus. Lisa continues to lick on Nick's penis and reaches for her phone.

Lisa looks at the screen and sees that the call is still connected. She starts to move her head up and down Nick's penis, making a loud slurping sound. Nick moans as Lisa quickens her pace and fights the urge to ejaculate. "Suck my cock baby! This feels so good!" he shouts much to Lisa's delight. She removes Nick's penis from her mouth and shouts, "Eat my pussy Nick! Eat it! I'm going to sit on your face!"

Nick smiles and spreads Lisa's legs so he can lick her vagina. Lisa starts to move her legs so she's rubbing her vagina on Nick's mouth while placing his penis back into her mouth. Lisa looks at her phone again from the corner of her eye and sees that the call is still connected. "Good, the call is still connected. I want Anna to hear everything that's going on here. I want her to know that Nick is my man!" Lisa thought.

Lisa continues to suck on Nick's penis. She begins to massage Nick's testicles with her hand, removes his penis from her mouth and sits up. She places her hand on Nick's penis and strokes it. Nick's legs tense as Lisa slowly then rapidly strokes his penis while licking his testicles. Nick adjusts his head so Lisa's buttocks doesn't prevent him from breathing. "You like this Nick? You like it when I sit on your face?" Lisa asks. Nick says, "Yes! I love eating your pussy!"

Lisa smiles and reaches for her phone, bringing it closer to them. She places the phone on the table next to the bed and moves her body so she can see Nick's face. Nick looks up at Lisa as she continues to rub her vagina on his mouth. He struggles to move his tongue in sequence with Lisa's hip movements, making Lisa laugh. "Nick, that tickles! I love the way you eat my pussy!" Lisa arches her back, showing off her firm, perky breasts. "Nick, tell me you want me. Tell me I'm better than Anna. Tell me my sweet pussy is better than Anna's old pussy!" Lisa shouts.

Nick is confused and shocked by Lisa's comments. He immediately removes his tongue from Lisa's vagina. "What? What are you talking about? How do you know Anna?" he asks. Lisa removes her hand from Nick's penis and slides her body so she can insert his penis into her vagina. Nick tries to hide his smile as he feels the warmth and tightness of Lisa's vagina. "I told you, tell me my young pussy is better than Anna's old pussy! She was married to my deceased lover and we fucked!" Lisa shouts.

Nick is in shock and disbelief. Lisa begins to ride on Nick's penis as he stares at her in shock. Lisa slaps Nick in the face and shouts, "Tell me my young pussy is better than Anna's old pussy! Tell me you want a young woman and not an old woman like Anna! Tell me that my pussy is yours! I want you to say it! Tell me now!"

Nick reluctantly starts to speak when Lisa leans over and kisses him passionately. Nick grabs Lisa's buttocks with his hands and squeezes them as he arches his body. He uses his hips and legs to rapidly thrust his penis into Lisa's vagina. Lisa moans loudly as Nick moves his hands to her hips. Lisa smiles as Nick takes control of her body and turns her over so he is now on top of her. Nick spreads Lisa's legs as he thrusts his penis inside of her vagina.

Lisa smiles and moans while Nick continues to thrust himself into her vagina. He grunts like an animal as he lies on top of her. Lisa shouts, "Nick, tell me, tell me! I want to hear it! Please tell me!" Nick shouts, "Your pussy is better than Anna's pussy! I love fucking your pussy!" and ejaculates inside of Lisa's vagina. He collapses on top of Lisa's sweaty body as Lisa gasps for air and tries to control her legs from shaking. Lisa holds Nick's head close to her breasts and slowly moves her hand over to her phone. She looks at the phone and says, "Good boy!" and ends the call.

XI Two Can Play...

Rays of sunlight shine on Anna's face as she tosses and turns on her bed. She knocks over several decorative pillows on to the floor and curls up into a fetal position. Anna turns over again, now lying on her back and the sunlight awakens her. "Goddammit! I can't get any sleep here in the morning ever since Jane changed the blinds on my windows! They let in too much of the sun! Now I can't go back to sleep!" Anna shouts.

Anna sits up in the bed, yawns and stretches her arms. A loud popping sound is made as she stretches. "I'm getting old" she thought as she turns to look at the alarm clock. "Oh God, it's only seven o'clock! That's it, those blinds go today! I'm going to have bags under my eyes because of this!" Anna says. Anna gets out of the bed and stretches her body, touching her toes, arching her back and bending her arms.

After Anna stretches, she turns to look at her alarm clock again and looks at her phone. She notices that a voicemail was left on her phone. Anna is confused by this and thought, "Who left me a message? Who called me last night? Oh yeah, Lisa called me when I was sleeping. I was so tired last night, I just ignored her call. I'm also tired of her bullshit and didn't want to talk to her. She probably drunk-dialed me or butt-dialed me. I'll listen to it later."

Anna goes into the bathroom and struggles to walk in a straight line. "I can't believe how sleepy I am! I still got 5 hours of sleep. I guess I need to get more now" she thought as she turns on the light. The ceiling light temporarily blinds Anna and she blinks her eyes so she can see. Anna continues her zombie-like walk towards the sink and slowly turns the knob labelled "Cold."

She cups her hands under the water and a cold chill runs down Anna's body.

Anna splashes the water on to her face and her eyes open widely from the freezing coldness of the water. She continues to splash water on to her face as she reaches for her toothbrush and toothpaste. Anna begins to brush her teeth and looks at herself in the mirror. As she brushes her teeth, she thought, "Why would Lisa call me so late? I never returned her calls and haven't spoken to her since that day we slept together. Who knows what she said? I'll listen to her message after this." Anna finishes brushing her teeth and rinses her mouth and toothbrush. She returns to the bedroom and stares at her phone. "Why am I hesitating? What am I afraid of? Just play the damn message already!" she thought.

Anna reaches for her phone and nervously presses the Voicemail button on the screen. The voicemail starts to play and Anna notices that the message is over 30 minutes long. "What the hell did she say? She must have butt-dialed me and later ended the call" Anna thought. Anna hears Lisa's voice as she shouts at someone, calling that person a "bitch." Lisa continues to shout at someone saying, "Finger my pussy" then Anna hears a familiar voice on the message.

Nick's voice is heard from Anna's phone, loud and clear enough to resonate throughout the room. Nick shouts, "Your pussy is better than Anna's pussy! I love fucking your pussy!" and Lisa says, "Good boy!" The message ends and Anna is in shock. Anna starts to cry and screams in anger. Her hands tremble in anger and Anna tries to control them. She clenches her fists and grinds her teeth in anger. "You fucking bitch! You little piece of shit! How dare you? How dare you do this to me? Ahh!" she shouts and collapses on the bed.

Anna punches her pillow repeatedly and sobs. Tears stream down her face on to the pillow and bed sheets, leaving watermarks on them. "How can she be so evil? It's one thing to seduce Nick, but to record it and send it to me! I can't believe she did that! You evil cunt! Oh you fucking little cunt! How dare you do this to me? I hate you!" Anna yells. She buries her head in a pillow and screams.

Anna screams for several minutes until her throat starts to hurt. She lifts her head from the pillow and breathes heavily. "Remember the breathing technique Sam showed you so you can calm down. I need to calm down. My heart feels like it's going to burst out of me" she thought. Anna starts to use the breathing technique that Sam taught her and starts to calm down. Her heart rate returns to normal and Anna feels at ease. Anna sits up in her bed and chuckles in disbelief.

Anna continues to breathe slowly until she calms down. She wipes away her tears and rubs her throat. "All of this screaming hurt my throat. I can't believe this little bitch did that. Was Nick also in on this mean joke? He didn't sound like he really wanted to say that. Lisa can be very aggressive and dominating. It wouldn't surprise me if she made Nick say that during sex, like some kind of sexual game. What do I do now? Nick wasn't too excited to talk to me earlier. He basically blew me off and then Lisa leaves that voicemail. Should I just say 'Fuck it' and move on or try to find out if Nick and I are really over?" Anna thought.

Anna gets up from her bed and goes into the bathroom. She walks over to the shower and turns on the water. Anna takes off her shirt and panties and gets into the shower, not waiting for the water to warm up. The cold water strikes Anna's body, sending a cold chill down her spine. Small goose bumps rise on her skin as she turns her body so the water can reach her back. Anna leans her head against the wall and cries. "She's so mean and vindictive! I'm not letting some little girl get the better of me! She wants to play games, I can play too!" Anna shouts.

Anna wipes away her tears and turns to face the shower head. She stands under the water and lifts her head so the water hits her face. Anna moves away from the stream of water and smiles.

"I know what I have to do! I will get Nick back! He's my man! I had him first and I still love him!" she says. Anna reaches for the bar of soap and begins to rub it until there is a layer of foam on the bar. She rubs the bar of soap on her body and an image of Nick enters her mind.

Nick is standing completely nude in her bedroom as she lies on the bed. Anna looks at Nick and says, "You really look good Nick. I can see that you've really been training hard. Come over here." Nick walks over to Anna and they kiss passionately. Anna moves her hands up and down Nick's body, rubbing his back and buttocks. Nick moves his tongue inside of Anna's mouth and she opens her mouth wider so he can insert his tongue deeper into her mouth.

Anna and Nick kiss for several minutes. Anna slowly moves her hand towards Nick's erect penis. "Looks like you're ready for me" Anna whispers. Nick says, "Yes baby, I want you. I want you now!" Anna lies back on the bed as Nick spreads her legs and kisses her feet. Anna laughs as Nick plants small kisses on her feet and then nibbles on them. Nick inserts his penis into Anna's vagina as she leans her head back and moans.

Nick holds Anna's legs apart as he thrusts himself into Anna's vagina. Anna's toes curl as Nick quickens his pace and thrusts his penis into her vagina over and over again. Anna shouts, "I'm cumming!" and Nick says, "I'm cumming too!" Anna shouts, "Cum inside of me!" Nick grunts loudly as he ejaculates inside of Anna's vagina. Anna smiles and realizes that her hand is by her vagina. She says, "Nick is mine and I'm getting him back!"

Anna rinses the soap off of her body, shuts off the water and exits the shower. Water drips off her body as Anna reaches for a towel. "I'm going to have to dry that up" she thought and wraps the towel around her body. Anna walks back to her bed, reaches for her phone and sits on the bed. Anna removes the towel from her body and presses the Camera button on her phone. "I'll show Nick what he's missing! I'll take, oh what's it called...a 'selfie' and send it to him" she thought.

Anna lies on her bed and holds her phone away from her body to take a picture. The phone falls out of her hand and Anna shouts, "Fuck! How the hell do these kids do this shit?" Anna leans over her bed to reach for her phone and almost slides off of the bed. Anna chuckles from nearly falling off of the bed and grabs her phone. She places her thumb securely where she has to press the button to take the picture and repositions herself on the bed.

Anna nervously lies on the bed, twisting her body so she can expose her breasts and smiles. She presses the button to take the picture and sits up. Anna quickly looks at the phone and reviews the picture. "Not bad for my first 'selfie'" she thought and lies back on the bed. She spreads her legs and holds the phone far from her body to take another picture. Anna looks at the picture and blushes. "I'm fucking hot!" Anna jokingly says and kneels on the bed. She extends her arms from her body and takes another picture, this one showing off her upper body and toned legs.

Anna stops taking pictures of herself and frowns. "I can't believe I'm doing this! I never had to do shit like this to get a man! Fucking kids! Well, if I want Nick back, I'm going to have to compete with Lisa or any other younger girl so this is what I have to do" she says and returns her focus to the phone. Anna gets on her hands and knees and holds the phone up in the air to take another picture. She looks at the picture and blushes again. "That's a good ass shot" she thought and chuckles. "One more should be good" Anna says, spreading her legs and arching her back so her vagina is exposed. She presses the button on the phone to take the picture and rolls over on to her back to look at the phone. "Wow! This looks like a photo shoot right out of Hustler Magazine!" Anna thought.

Anna presses the Photos button on the phone and slides her finger across the screen to review the pictures. She nods her head in approval of each photo and presses the Menu button on the phone. Anna presses Share and presses Messaging, scrolling through her Contacts list, stopping at Nick's name. She presses Nick's name and his name and phone number appear in the "To" field of the message. Anna attaches the pictures to the message and types, "I just wanted to remind you what you're missing out on. I miss you and want to see you."

Anna pauses before pressing the Send button and looks at herself in the mirror. "Do I really want to do this? What if this doesn't work? I'll be the old woman who's trying to act like I'm still in my 20's! No! I want Nick back!" she says. She looks at the message on the phone and says, "That sounds too desperate!" Anna hits the Backspace button on phone until the message is gone. Anna pauses again then types, "Come and get it...I'm waiting. Anna." Anna presses the Send button and waits as the message uploads the photos and "Message Sent" is displayed on the screen. She sighs and says, "Now it's a waiting game" and lies back on the bed.

Nick tosses and turns as he tries to sleep. He winces in pain as Lisa's knee is planted in the small of his back. "Fuck that's annoying! If this turns into a long-term thing, we're going to have to talk about the sleeping arrangements!" he thought. Lisa lies next to him sound asleep with her mouth open. She snores loudly as she turns her body and hits Nick with her elbow. "Damn! Am I sleeping or fighting? She gets to sleep while I get beaten up here! If I wasn't so tired, I would have left after we fucked!" he thought.

Nick slowly gets out of the bed and stretches, wincing in pain. "My lower back really hurts! She must have hit me really hard with that knee! Just shake it off Nick! I'll freshen up, go back to my place and sleep. I've earned a week off and I intend on making the most of it" he thought. Nick puts on his clothes and staggers into the bathroom. He sits on the toilet bowl and reaches for his phone. Nick looks at the phone and sees, "1 New

Message" displayed on the screen. He presses the envelope icon on the screen and smiles when the message is displayed.

Nick scrolls through the pictures Anna sent him and smiles. His smile widens as he looks at each picture that Anna sent, one being more provocative than the previous one. "Holy shit!" Nick says and stops himself from speaking so he doesn't wake Lisa. He pauses for a moment and hears Lisa snoring, letting out a sigh of relief. "I didn't wake her, good!" he thought and returns his focus to the phone.

Nick reviews each picture that Anna sent him. He whispers, "Damn! Anna's fucking hot! She's great in bed, just as good, if not better than Lisa, but I never thought she'd do this! She barely knows how to use her phone, let alone take a 'selfie!' I guess being the Champ has its advantages" and smiles. Lisa's snores can still be heard from the bathroom and Nick chuckles. "Damn! Lisa sounds like a chainsaw! I'll wash up, call the driver and go home" he thought. Nick turns on the water from the sink, cupping his hands under the water and splashes his face with water.

Nick looks at himself in the mirror and smiles. "I've never had two women want me at the same time. I just had a great time with Lisa, but I still care about Anna. We have a history together and I only know Lisa for a short period of time. I don't know what to do here. I have to admit, Anna's pictures really do it for me and if she was here, I'd fuck her brains out. Those pictures just made me want Anna that much more" he thought.

Nick pauses and looks around to see if Lisa is awake. He whispers, "OK, she's still asleep." Nick continues to wash his face. "Yes, I thought with my dick last night and fucked Lisa, but I really wanted Anna. I was still angry at her and fucked Lisa out of spite. Instead of doing that, I'm listening to the 'chainsaw' over there. Jesus Christ! Lisa's so fucking loud! I'll head home and call Anna from the car. Maybe all of this drama may finally end" he thought.

Nick turns off the water, reaches for a towel and dries his face. He slowly tiptoes out of the bathroom, goes into the living room and finds a notepad and pen by the cordless phone. Nick tears a sheet off of the pad and writes, "Lisa, I have to go. I had a great time last night and would like to see you again. I'll call you later. Nick." He takes a piece of tape from the tape dispenser and places the note on to the back of the door.

Nick slowly turns the lock and the doorknob, opening the door so he can exit the apartment. "This is so cliché, but this is the only way I can get out of here. I know if I wake up Lisa, she'll want me to stay or start some drama about me leaving. I don't want to deal with that" he thought. Nick gently closes the door and calls the driver as he walks down the hallway. "OK, you'll be here in five minutes? Great!" Nick says and ends the call.

Nick stands in front of the building and nervously looks through the glass doors, hoping that Lisa doesn't come out. The car arrives and Nick quickly enters the car. The car drives away from Lisa's building and Nick exhales. "Good! I got away without any drama! Now I can relax and get some rest" Nick says. The driver chuckles and says, "Champ, I know exactly where you're coming from. Women can be too dramatic at times!" Nick smiles and yes, "Yeah, I hear you."

Nick looks at his phone and looks at the pictures that Anna sent to him earlier. A wide grin appears on Nick's face as he stares at Anna's pictures and he licks his lips. Nick leans back in the seat and presses the Call button on the screen. He scrolls down to Anna's name and presses on it. Anna's picture is displayed on the screen as Nick listens to the ringing on the phone. The phone rings for several minutes and Anna answers.

Nick eagerly waits for Anna to answer his call. "Hopefully she's awake. It's not even 8 o'clock, but I want to talk to her, especially now" he thought. Anna answers the call and Nick says, "Hi Anna, it's Nick. How are you?" Anna tries to hide her excitement and says, "I'm OK. I got out of the shower a few minutes ago. I guess you got my message?" Nick smiles and says, "Yes, I got it. All I have to say is, 'Wow!' Anna, you look amazing! I can't believe you sent those to me! I thought you'd never do something like this! Wow!"

Anna smiles as Nick continues to compliment her pictures. She lies back on her bad, propping up her pillows to support her head. "I knew it! I knew that would work! That little bitch thought she could take Nick from me! He's coming back to me!" she thought. Nick says, "Anna, I'm sorry that I sounded...I mean...I was rude to you earlier. I didn't mean that. I just finished getting undressed and had a lot going on." Nick pauses and thought, "I hope she believes me. Last night was a mistake and I want her back."

Anna smirks at Nick's comment and smiles. "He doesn't know that Lisa called me and recorded them having sex. Interesting..." she thought. Anna smiles and says, "That's OK. I understand. As long as you called me and explained everything, that's OK. What are you doing now?" Nick removes the phone from his ear and pauses. He smiles and thought, "Oh shit! Anna wants me to come over! I've never been with two different women on the same day, one after the other! Now I know what these guys are talking about!"

Nick puts the phone his ear and speaks. "I'm not really doing anything now. You want me to stop by? I mean, can I stop by to see you?" he says. The driver tries to stop his laughter as Nick eagerly waits for Anna's answer. Anna smiles and says, "Sure, come on over. I'll be waiting" and ends the call. Nick whispers, "Yes!" and puts his phone away. The driver gives Nick a "thumbs up" and Nick laughs.

Nick asks the driver to take him to Anna's house and the driver makes a turn to go to Anna's house. He leans back in his seat and says, "It's great being the Champ!" and both he and the driver laugh. Anna puts her phone down, smiles and says, "I got you now! Nick is mine!" and goes into the bathroom to prepare for Nick's arrival.

XII Have Your Cake and Eat it Two

Anna looks at herself in the full-length mirror and examines herself. She turns her body so she can look at herself from different angles. Anna smiles as she poses in front of the mirror. Anna nods approvingly after posing in the mirror and smiles. "I knew Nick would come back to me! How can he pass up on a hit piece of ass like this?" she says and playfully smacks her buttocks.

Anna moves over to the sink and washes her face. After she washes her face, Anna looks at herself in the mirror. She stares at her reflection in the mirror and frowns. She says, "If I didn't care about Nick so much, I wouldn't be throwing myself at him like this! It's usually the other way around. Men usually chase me! Well, bottom line is, I'm the winner! Nick is coming here to see me! That little bitch Lisa tried to take Nick from me and she failed!"

Anna dries her face and looks at herself in the mirror again. She applies some concealer on her face, some red lipstick to her lips and curls her eyelashes. "Now I'm ready for Nick" she thought and exits the bathroom. Anna uses her hands to flatten the sheets on the bed and fluffs up the pillows, preparing for Nick's arrival. She goes into her dresser drawer and takes out a purple g-string thong with matching bra.

Anna slides her legs through the thong and decides not to put on the bra. "I think that just wearing the g-string is hot enough. The bra will just get in the way" she thought. Anna puts the bra back into the drawer and quickly closes the drawer when the doorbell rings. A rush of excitement fills her body and she jumps back from the dresser. "He's here!" Anna shouts and quickly reaches for her robe. She runs down the stairs to the living room.

Nick stands in front of Anna's house and sweats nervously. "I hope Anna can't tell that I was with Lisa earlier. I did freshen myself up a little, but I didn't have time for a shower. I can't believe this is happening! Two women, one after the other! This is so fucking cool!" he thought. Nick rings the doorbell and can hear Anna's footsteps as she runs down the stairs. "She always was heavy footed. If she tried to steal something or sneak out, she'd be too loud to get away" he thought.

Anna opens the door and smiles at Nick. Nick smiles and says, "I'm here, as promised. God, you look great!" He stares at Anna and thought, "Anna looks amazing!" Anna stands in the doorway with her robe partially open, showing off her long legs and pedicured feet. Nick stares at Anna, admiring her body and Anna grabs Nick by his shirt. She says, "There's more to see inside" and pulls him into the house.

Nick stumbles into the living room, surprised at Anna's strength. "I would have walked in if you asked honey!" Nick jokingly says as Anna closes the door. Anna turns around, takes off her robe and kisses Nick on the neck. She bites Nick's neck while grabbing his buttocks with both of her hands. Nick winces in pain form Anna biting him and slowly moves his hands down Anna's body.

Anna continues to kiss Nick as he holds her. "I'm going to do whatever it takes to win Nick back! That little cunt will not claim my man! Nick is mine!" she thought. Nick caresses her buttocks and says, "Baby, I love the way your ass feels and looks!" He bends down and kisses Anna's buttocks, planting several kisses on both cheeks. Anna laughs and says, "You better save your energy, we're just getting started." Nick playfully smacks Anna's right cheek as he kisses and sucks on the left cheek of her buttocks. He purposely leaves a red mark on Anna's left cheek and says, "I'm marking my territory" and Anna chuckles saying, "I'm all yours."

Nick begins to kiss Anna's right side of her buttocks while Anna giggles. "That tickles!" Anna says and Nick uses his teeth to grab on to the g-string of Anna's thong. He slowly pulls Anna's thong down her legs and Anna smiles. Anna lifts her legs one at a time so Nick can completely remove her thong and playfully tosses it across the living room.

Anna and Nick lie on the floor kissing passionately. They hold each other closely, enjoying the warmth from their bodies. Nick slides off his shoes one at a time and thought, "Thank God for penny loafers! I don't want to stop this just to untie a fucking shoe!" Anna unbuckles Nick's belt and Nick arches his body so he can slide his pants and boxers off of his body. Anna takes off Nick's shirt and lies on top of Nick's naked body.

Anna lies on top of Nick as they kiss. She slowly moves her hand down from Nick's chest to his abdomen and thought, "Wow, Nick really toned down for that fight! I can feel how hard his stomach is! That's so sexy!" Anna moves her had towards Nick's penis and begins to stroke it up and down. Nick holds Anna's head as he moves his tongue in her mouth while she continues to stroke his penis. Nick removes his hands from Anna's head and she asks, "Do you still love me?"

Anna looks at Nick intensely as she waits for his answer. "If he stalls or pauses, then he's lying. I'm not going to throw myself at Nick if he doesn't love me" she thought. Nick looks at Anna and says, "I do love you. I love you very much. I love you so much that I have to be honest and tell you something." Anna looks at Nick with a blank stare and sits up.

Anna removes her hand from Nick's penis and gets off of his body. Nick sits up and says, "Anna, last night was one of the most memorable nights of my life. I never thought I'd win the title, let alone get a title shot. Before you called me, a girl I dated after we broke up called and wanted to see me. Ironically, she also sent me nude 'selfies' and I agreed to meet her. Her name is

Lisa. It's weird. She made me shout out things about you while we had sex? Do you know her?"

Anna looks at Nick and slaps him. Nick opens his mouth to speak and Anna kisses him. He is confused and speechless. They kiss passionately for several minutes and Nick stops kissing Anna. He asks, "What was that for? Why the hell did you do that? I was being honest with you! I don't want to be with anyone else now. I only want you!"

Tears begin to flow from Anna's eyes and she says, "I know all about Lisa! She's the girl that had an affair with Paul! I also slept with her before I came to your place the last time we saw each other! It was a huge mistake that I regret. I'm just happy that she's no longer going to interfere in our lives and we can be together! I only want you!"

Nick looks at Anna and his eyes begin to tear up. "Anna I don't want to lose you either. You mean so much to me. I love you." Anna and Nick hug and she whispers, "You want to go to the bedroom?" Nick says, "I thought you'd never ask" and smiles. Anna says, "OK, you go ahead, I'll lock the door and follow you." Nick jogs up the stairs as Anna walks over to the door to lock it. As Anna locks the door and lifts the chain to place it in its slot, the doorbell rings. Anna looks through the peephole and is shocked when she sees who standing there.

Anna is in complete shock when she sees Lisa standing on the opposite side of the door. "What the fuck is she doing here?" Anna shouts. Nick hears Anna's shouting and immediately runs down the stairs. Nick runs up to Anna and asks, "What's wrong?" Anna continues to stare at Lisa through the peephole and says, "That fucking whore is here! She's in front of my fucking house! First she records you two having sex and now she has the balls to come here! Fuck that little bitch!"

Before Nick can speak, Anna grabs the doorknob and opens the door. She grabs Lisa and pulls her into the living room. Lisa staggers into the living room and almost falls down. Nick catches

Lisa and stands her upright. Anna closes the door and locks it. "Oh my God! I made a mistake coming here! Anna looks like she wants to kill me!" Lisa thought. Lisa trembles in fear as Anna looks at her with a vicious stare.

Nick walks over to Anna so he's by her side. Lisa looks at the floor and says, "I didn't expect Nick to be here." Lisa looks at Nick and says, "You left my place without even saying 'Goodbye.' I thought you were going home. Now I see that you want both of us." Lisa looks at Nick in disgust as she points at his erect penis. Nick blushes and looks at the floor. Anna angrily swats her hand away.

Nick notices that he is completely naked. He runs over to where his pants and boxers are lying on the floor. Nick quickly puts on his boxers as Anna confronts Lisa. "What the fuck are you doing here? You have some nerve coming here! How did you find out where I live?" Anna asks. Anna bends down to get her robe while Lisa tries to stop trembling in fear.

Lisa avoids looking at Anna so she can stop trembling. As she tries to stop shaking, Lisa says, "I had your address when I was with Paul. You did catch us here when we were together." Anna puts on her robe and dismissively says, "OK, fine. Why are you here?" Lisa momentarily looks at Nick and Anna shouts, "Don't look at Nick! Answer me!" Anna's voice booms as she shouts "Don't look at Nick! Answer me!"

Lisa returns her attention to Anna as she continues to tremble in fear. She looks at Anna and notices that both of Anna's hands are clenched into fists. "I don't want to get hurt. Oh please don't hurt me" Lisa says. She starts to cry and says, "I wanted to say 'I'm sorry' to you. I had to tell you this face to face." Lisa tries to stop crying and pauses to wipe her tears.

Anna looks at Lisa and tries not to feel pity for her. "I don't care if she's sorry. I want her out of here!" she thought. Lisa looks at Anna and says, "You didn't deserve to be treated the way I treated you. I took your husband from you, I slept with your boyfriend, tried to hurt you with that phone call and seduced you. After all of the shit you've been through...you still stand strong. You still get the man in the end. You still win! I hate and admire you at the same time!"

Anna looks at Lisa and starts to cry. Lisa begins to sob and Anna walks over to her. Lisa flinches as Anna approaches her, fearing that Anna will harm her. Anna slowly extends her arms and wraps them around Lisa's body. Lisa stops trembling in fear as Anna brings her close to her body and holds her. Lisa tearfully says, "I'm so sorry! I'm so sorry that I did all of those terrible things to you! I'm sorry I hurt you! I just...I just..."

Lisa stops speaking and kisses Anna on the lips. Anna allows Lisa to kiss her as Nick watches in shock. Nick watches them kiss and thought, "What the fuck is going on here? I feel like I'm in some kind of TV novella on Galavisíon! Hopefully all of this drama will end soon and Lisa will leave. I really want to go upstairs with Anna and continue where we left off. Lisa coming here was the LAST thing I thought could happen. I thought Anna was going to beat the shit out of Lisa."

After consoling Lisa for several minutes, Anna pulls away from Lisa. Lisa kisses Anna on the lips one more time before Anna pulls away from her. Anna looks at Lisa and says, "I forgive you. I forgive you." Lisa whispers, "Thank you" and kisses Anna on the lips again. Anna returns Lisa's kiss and they continue kissing. Nick stares at Anna and Lisa as they kiss and thought, "Holy shit! Who would have seen this coming? Damn this is hot!" as his penis slowly becomes erect.

Anna begins to remove Lisa's jacket while Lisa slides off her flip-flops and pajama bottoms. Nick continues to stare at them as Anna removes Lisa's clothes and his penis begins to stick out of his boxers. He thought, "This is too fucking hot! I want both of them! I know it's selfish, but I can't ignore what's happening here. Anna and Lisa are so beautiful and they look like they want each other. I want them too! I want them now!"

Nick walks up behind Anna and starts kissing her neck while slowly removing her robe. Lisa removes her bra while Anna tries to remove her panties. Nick notices that Anna is having some difficulty removing Lisa's panties and squats behind Anna. He slowly removes Lisa's panties and she lifts her legs one at a time so he can take them off. Anna and Lisa pause to look at Nick squatting down on the floor and both smile.

Anna and Lisa return their attention to each other and continue to kiss. Nick looks up at Anna and stares at her as she kisses Lisa. He thought, "This is really happening! I'm going to have a threesome! Enough of this foreplay shit, I want to go upstairs!" Nick stands up and removes his boxers so they are all naked. He pulls Anna and Lisa apart, kissing Anna then kisses Lisa. He looks at both of them and asks, "Ladies, shall we go upstairs?" Anna and Lisa look at each other, smile and turn to Nick. They say in unison, "Yes" and Nick smiles. Anna and Lisa run up the stairs towards the bedroom and Nick thought, "Everyone wants to be with the Champ" and runs up the stairs with a wide grin on his face.

FIN

Also by Alejandro Morales

Standalone
Cougar
Cougar II Triangle of Lust

About the Author

Alejandro Morales was born and raised in Brooklyn, NY. During his youth, he read the works of Stephen King and Anne Rice, influencing his writing style. Alejandro likes to incorporate different aspects of his personality into his characters and writing, making his work both entertaining and provocative. He is currently working on several projects and marketing his first book, Cougar for on-screen production.

Made in the USA
Middletown, DE
04 June 2015